D0297773

BF

She snaked her arms around his waist, then laid her cheek on his back—on the cold fur of his parka. In spite of the brisk temperature, she felt a spark of heat.

His or hers? She didn't know, but the instant her arms reached around him she felt it, and it was enough to keep her warm. A nice warmth, and not so much about staving off the cold as it was about the proximity to Michael.

"Now, hold on tight, because I don't go back for anyone that bumps off."

He didn't have to ask her twice to hold on tight. She'd been this route before and knew all the bumps intimately. Of course there was a new bump tonight—the one bumping double-speed in her chest. And she knew it wasn't about the impending ride. Not in the least.

Now that her children have finally left home, **Dianne Drake** finally has time to do some of the things she loves—gardening, cooking, reading, shopping for antiques, going to the symphony. Her absolute passion in life, however, is adopting abandoned and abused animals. Right now Dianne and her husband Joel have a little menagerie, consisting of three dogs and two cats, but that's always subject to change. Dianne loves to hear from readers, so feel free to e-mail her at DianneDrake@earthlink.net

Recent titles by the same author:

MEDICINE MAN
THE SURGEON'S RESCUE MISSION
THE DOCTOR'S COURAGEOUS BRIDE

EMERGENCY IN ALASKA

BY
DIANNE DRAKE

MILLS & BOON®

To my old pal Gary, a great doctor who found
his true love in the wilds of Alaska.

First published in Great Britain 2006
Large Print edition 2007
Harlequin Mills & Boon Limited,
Eton House, 18-24 Paradise Road,
Richmond, Surrey TW9 1SR

© Dianne Drake 2006

ISBN-13: 978 0 263 19531 6
ISBN-10:   0 263 19531 7

Set in Times Roman 16½ on 19 pt.
17-0107-55649

Printed and bound in Great Britain
by Antony Rowe Ltd, Chippenham, Wiltshire

CHAPTER ONE

"SO THIS is where nowhere begins," Michael Morse grumbled, turning the map over a couple of times, looking for something on it that would tell him which way to go, then finally giving up. Impatiently, he wadded it into a ball then chucked it into the rear of his Jeep, and leaned forward against the steering wheel, looking up at the sky. "Like charting the clouds is going to get me somewhere," he muttered, spotting the ominously dark one hanging directly over him. He'd been lost a good two hours now, not sure if he was going round in circles, advancing in any particular direction or even backtracking over terrain he'd previously traveled. "She's out of her mind," he muttered. "Totally out of her mind."

Sighing, he took a look at the desolate white road stretching out to eternity ahead of him, then twisted around and looked at the exact same road behind him. "How the hell did you even find a place like this, let alone decide to stay here?" A little holiday to Alaska was what she'd told him.

Brilliant idea, he'd thought. She'd been so lonely this past year since his dad had died, and she deserved a new life. But in Alaska? Specifically, Elkhorn, Alaska, population fluctuating somewhere near the five-hundred mark. "You have more people living in your condominium complex. *I* have more people than that come through my emergency-room door every week. Totally, unequivocally ridiculous," he grunted, glancing around again.

And here he was, at this particular crossroads, coming from nowhere, going to nowhere, doubting not only her sanity at this juncture but his own for chasing after his mother in this godforsaken sweep of nowhere. "She is a grown woman, after all. Respected surgeon, traveled, capable of taking care of herself." But she was his mother, and that was that. He had to look after her. "Even when you do something this… this…crazy, Maggie!"

Michael assessed his choices again, hoping that somehow he'd missed one—the best one, whatever that might be. Still, every which way he looked, the only things looming ahead, behind or to the sides were endless strips of narrow, rutted, icy roads lined by snow-capped trees. Lots of them. And not one of them with a road sign tacked to it telling him which icy road to take or, for that matter, which icy road *not* to take.

Which meant that he was lost. Or, if not lost, so vastly confused that no matter which way he chose, he would soon be lost. Even worse, soon to be without petrol if he wasn't careful about this.

Alone, in the Alaskan wilds, without gasoline. Not a good spot in which to be, since there was no way of knowing when the next human being might come along, or where the next tiny dot calling itself a town would be located and if that dot would even have a gasoline pump. "She can't be up here," he grunted. "Can't be, wouldn't be. She's got better sense than that." But the e-mail he'd received just over a week ago had specifically stated she was staying in Elkhorn, which was somewhere near Moosejaw, and up the road from Bear Creek. Not only that, she was living with a man named Dimitri.

Michael wasn't sure which was worse, that his

mother was living in Alaska, or that she was living with a man…in Alaska.

Dimitri—a name that conjured up some definite images. Big, burly… "This isn't the way I wanted to spend my holiday, Mom," he shouted at the top of his lungs, immediately feeling a little silly about sitting out there in the middle of nowhere shouting at nothing but open space and trees. But time off from the hospital was precious. He didn't get much of it, and when he did manage to put together a few days away, he preferred a nice beach somewhere. *And not on the Alaskan coast.*

But she was so vulnerable now. And who wouldn't be, after losing a spouse of forty years? "Except most people don't take their vulnerability to Alaska," he grunted, looking up at the hawk circling overhead. "Right into the arms of someone called Dimitri Romonov," he shouted at the bird, who squawked a protest over having his peace disturbed, then flew off, leaving Michael feeling even more alone than before.

"Dr. Dimitri Romonov." His lip nearly curled as he spoke the name. The man was simply taking advantage of a woman at a loose end. "That's all it could be," he said aloud as he pulled out the crumpled map, took another look at it, then re-crumpled it and fixed his attention on a rabbit darting out of the bushes. "Okay, if I were a town called Elkhorn, where would I be?" he asked it, only to watch it duck right back into the bushes when he spoke. "Or even Moosejaw," he called after it. "Right now I'd be elated with Moosejaw." As the last of the rabbit's white undertail disappeared, Michael stepped out of the Jeep and looked around, not that it would do him any good. But doing something sure beat sitting there doing nothing. At least this way he got in a good stretch, and at six feet four inches, his long legs needed that. That, and a brisk walk straight up to the front door of a man named Dimitri.

"Okay, I'll admit it. I'm lost. *Lost!*" he shouted, as he wandered into the middle of the four-way ice-slick that passed for an intersection. He took a good look in every direction, trying to see if there was one of the intersecting roads that appeared more traveled than another. Deeper ruts in the ice, maybe. Less of a snow pack off to the side. Things he taught his wilderness students to look for. "Looks like the teacher fails the course," he muttered, when he couldn't find a discernible difference anywhere around him. "Hundreds of doctors certified, and the teacher can't practice what he preaches."

In the middle of the intersection, Michael turned in a complete circle, little by little, looking for anything that might point him to civilization. While his back was turned toward his Jeep, and his attention fixed on the road straight ahead, another Jeep came crashing onto the road, apparently from a fire trail or access road, and whooshed right into the intersection. "What the…?" he started as he felt the rush of cold air hit his face when the Jeep skidded within a few meters of him, then slid in a complete circle on a thin snowy patch, trying to come to a stop. Anyway, it looked like it was trying to stop because it did two more pirouettes before it landed front end down in a shallow, snowy ditch right across from his own Jeep.

"What do you think you're doing?" the driver screamed at him as she scrambled out to assess her situation. "Trying to get yourself killed? And me? I could have been killed here, you know!" She ran to the front of her Jeep, bent down to one knee and took a look underneath. Then she stood, looked up the incline at him, opened her mouth to say something, stared for several seconds and shut her mouth.

"You're not hurt, are you?" he asked, although he doubted she was, not with the way she was acting.

"No, I'm not…" she began rather hesitantly, then shook her head and sucked in a deep breath. "So what are you doing still standing there? Waiting for someone else to come along and run over you? Which they will if you don't move, and which you'll deserve if they do! And don't expect me to stay around here to pick up the pieces, because I don't have time!"

Instinctively, Michael stepped back instead of forward. "Are you sure you're okay?" he asked, wondering if he should assess her for a head injury. A good slosh to the brain could cause a violent reaction like she was having. He saw it all the time. One bonk and instant personality change. "Didn't hit your head or anything?" He thought her pupils looked equal and reactive but he wasn't close enough to tell, and he wasn't sure he wanted to get close enough. Out here, in the middle of nowhere with a madwoman…

"You think I have a concussion?"

"If you hit your head…"

"I'm fine, no thanks to you, standing in the middle of the road like an idiot. So, are you going to diagnose me, or push me out of the ditch?"

"Push you out? You expect me to push you out? If you hadn't been driving like a crazy woman you wouldn't have ended up down there in the first place, so don't go blaming me for your bad driving, lady, because I'm the innocent by-stander here." He took another step backward. "And it's your fault you're in a ditch. Not mine."

"And it's going to be your fault, not mine, when I take your Jeep and leave you stranded out here. And I *will* take your Jeep. So here's your choice. You push, I drive, or I drive and you stay. Take your pick." She shoved back her fur Cossack hat, and looked up at him. "So what's it going to be?"

From what he could tell looking down at her, she was tall. Maybe five eight or five nine. And under all her bulk—the red plaid jacket, the fur hat—she might have been curvy, but he couldn't see for sure, and he wasn't going in for a closer look. "Okay, I'll push, but I don't owe you a damn thing," he snorted. "The way you were driving, you're lucky it's only a ditch you ended up in and not an emergency room." As director of an emergency department, he saw the sad results of reckless driving like hers every day. Devastating injuries, permanent disabilities, death. Somehow, though, he associated that kind of driving with the city. Apparently careless and foolhardy driving was the same everywhere, including somewhere in the far or, he hoped, near vicinity of Elkhorn.

"You're lucky it's only a ditch I ended up in, too. Because if it was anything more…"

"Yeah, I know. You'd have already taken my Jeep and left me out here alone." She was a pushy thing, too. Cheeky and pushy, and he was betting that if he could make out her features under that big hat she was wearing, which he could not, he'd see pure fire there. "But I am curious why you think you could get my Jeep away from me."

"Because I'm on an emergency and you're not. And I have police powers when I need to use them." To emphasize her point, she hiked up her coat, pulled a wallet from her pocket and showed him her badge.

"Got handcuffs?" he asked, trying to fight back a smile. For all her put-on fierceness, it simply wasn't in her eyes. Fire, yes. Anger, absolutely. But she wasn't a bully. Just someone pretending to be, and he wasn't falling for that. Except it was cute, in an odd sort of way. Not his type in a woman, though, but out here the only type he really wanted to see was one with directions to the Romonov Clinic where his mother had said she was taking up medical practice. "So I'll push. And in return, you'll tell me how to get to Elkhorn."

"I'll put it in Reverse," she hissed, swinging herself up into her Jeep. "You get down here and push when I tell you to. But stay off to the side because I don't want to—"

"I know. You don't want to pick up the pieces because you don't have time." Amazingly, he liked that little bit of impatience in her. It was real. She wasn't trying to make a good impression. Good thing, because she wasn't.

Instead of answering, she gunned her engine impatiently as Michael took his place at the front and side of her Jeep. The first two attempts to rock her backward were futile because she was nosed down pretty steep into the ditch and he didn't have a good foothold in the snow. But the third attempt, after he'd dug his foot in all the way to the frozen earth, tilted her back sufficiently that she made it out of the ditch and straight back into the road, spinning almost out of control then sliding in reverse on the ice so fast she nearly smashed straight into the side of his Jeep. By the time she'd slammed on her brakes and spun around in a full circle, twice, she was less than a meter away from ramming right into the driver's side door of his rental, where she finally slid to a stop. "Really stupid place to park your car," she yelled, instead of, *Thank you for the help.*

Somehow, though, that's exactly what he'd expected from her. "I don't know what kind of police powers you pack, lady, but someone ought to take away your driver's license because if you don't kill yourself, you're going to kill someone else. And I sure as hell hope it isn't me."

"Won't be you if you don't stand in the middle of the intersection," she retorted, pulling forward, then turning her vehicle to head in the original direction in which she'd been traveling.

"So where's Elkhorn?" he called, climbing his way from the ditch up onto the road. "Or any other reasonable facsimile of civilization, or even a gas pump?"

She peered out from under her hat at him again. "What do you want in Elkhorn?" she asked, tilting her head enough that he finally got his first good look at her face.

Surprisingly cute. Not so surprisingly angry. And definitely ready to run over him if she had to. To think that his mother had said the people out here were friendly. Apparently she'd never met this spitfire, who was already gunning her engine for the takeoff. Heaven help the people down the road if they didn't get out of her way. "Elkhorn. Simple directions to the clinic in Elkhorn. That's all I want."

"You've got to be kidding!" she sputtered, looking up at him, then shaking her head adamantly. "And I thought he had better sense than that. When he told me he was thinking about… No. He wouldn't. He…" She drew in a discomposed breath, then blew it out in a puff of white vapor into the crisp Arctic air. "Look, I don't have time to waste sitting here like this, talking to you. And you've already cost me five minutes I didn't have in the first place."

"I wasn't aware that's what we were doing," he said, not sure whether to be amused by her or to run for his life. "Sitting here, talking. It's more like I'm standing in the middle of the road begging for simple directions, and you're sitting in the Jeep yelling at me or, in the worst-case scenario, threatening to steal my vehicle. And muttering to yourself. Where I come from we avoid people like that." But she did have a nice voice. A little bit low, reasonably throaty. The kind of voice he liked to hear in the bedroom, on the brink of sex, when it got all husky and full of excitement. Except her voice was definitely not excited.

"Well, avoid me next time you see me. Okay?"

"I'll be happy to avoid you *right now* if you'll tell me where I can find Elkhorn."

"That way," she said, pointing so quickly in a direction that he didn't catch on. "Left, then first right, take another right at the red barn, and another at the rusty pickup truck, go ten more kilometers and veer to the left when you see Dowiak's pond, which does have a sign. Stay on that road until you come to the three-way, take the road to the left, and another left at the boulder—you can't miss it since it's in the middle of the road, and that road will take you straight into Elkhorn."

"Could you write that down?" he asked, reasonably sure she would not. "Starting with the red barn?"

Instead of answering, she huffed out another exasperated breath, took a firm grip on the steering wheel with her gloved hands and shook her head impatiently. "Don't have time for this, don't have time for you. Milt Furman usually makes a run through here later in the day with the mail. I'll send a relay out to have him lead you on in. If he doesn't, I'll be back by here later tonight." She glanced up at the forbidding sky, and frowned. "Or you can follow me to Beaver Dam right now and get to Elkhorn when I go there later on." Without another word, she put her Jeep into gear and shot off down the icy road that went to the right.

Michael stood in the intersection for another

second debating his options, which were precious few—stay there lost until Milt whatever-his-name-was happened by, wait until the road demon came back, or follow her now and hope for the best. "Why not?" he muttered, then ran back to his own Jeep, hopped in and sped down the same road. "Why the hell not?" At least she had a known destination. That was better than his having only a town name without directions to it and a sure knowledge that he *didn't* want to spend any more time lost on an isolated road in the cold.

No, he wasn't sure where he was going, or who this crazy lady was he was following, but Beaver Dam was apparently in his foreseeable future, and maybe somebody there could draw him a map to Elkhorn. Or fill his gas tank so he could spend another few hours wandering aimlessly in the Alaskan wilderness looking for the boulder in the road, as well as his mother.

"You owe me for this one, Maggie Morse," he muttered as he spotted the other Jeep ahead and set his speed to follow it at a safe distance—a very safe distance with the way she was driving. "You really owe me in a big way for this one."

CHAPTER TWO

DR. ALEKSANDRA SOKOLOV took a hasty glance into her rear-view mirror and heaved yet another a deep, irritated sigh when she saw that he was following right along. Of all the people in the world Dimitri could have hired to come and work with them, he had to go and hire him. Dr. Michael Morse! Sure, Dimitri had mentioned a name…Dr. Morris, or Dr. Morrison, or something like that, she'd thought. She hadn't been paying much attention since she'd been preparing to leave for a conference. But if she had heard Dr. *Morse*, particularly Dr. *Michael* Morse…well, she wasn't sure what she would have done, but it would have started with a list of reasons not to hire the last man she ever wanted to see again, let alone work with!

She drew in a deep, calming breath, trying to put him…put that whole offensive incident out of her head, stunned by how, after all this time, she still had such a strong reaction to him.

He was Chief of Emergency Services at Seattle North, and a professor at the medical school. He wrote books on wilderness medicine and he lectured all around the world on the subject. He also taught certification classes—taught *her* certification class, actually. He also did television interviews whenever someone was lost in the wilderness and the reporters flocked to him for an expert speculation on how long a person could last under certain conditions, in certain weather, at a certain time of the year.

Michael Morse had his reputation and it was well earned, so why someone like that would come here to practice medicine in a fifty-bed clinic in the middle of nowhere, for practically no money, when he had everything where he was, was beyond her. Researching another book? Big-city burnout? Scorned lover on his tail? Adding a notch of humility and altruism to his curriculum vitae? Whatever the reason, Dimitri would offer him a room, food, a lot more hours of work than he'd ever done in his life, and a barely livable stipend that might keep him in warm clothes if he knew how to budget his stipend wisely. And none of that was Michael Morse's style medically, socially or otherwise. *Why here? Why her?* Quite simply, she didn't want to work with the great Dr. Morse. Not after what he'd done to her.

The only problem was, he was following her right now. Keeping up, probably quite pleased with himself over how easily he was doing it. She smiled, thinking about how easy it would be to veer off onto one of the old fire roads and lose him. Problem was bears. He was a soft, spoiled city boy and she was betting that he didn't even have enough common sense to come out here with a good bear repellant. She chuckled. City boys in particular were tasty and tender to the bears. "I should do it," she said, glancing back again. "I really should." But there was an outbreak of some sort in Beaver Dam, and since he was already halfway there, there was no sense in letting his medical skills go to waste.

Alek thought about the call that had come in. She'd been down in Nome restocking supplies for a few days, just up from Juneau after a nice week at a medical conference, when Dimitri's relay had got through to her. Up here, the phone service wasn't always as convenient as it was in the cities. And in some places there was no cell-phone service whatsoever. But the relay never let you down—you'd call someone who would, in turn, get through to someone else who would then call or radio another person until the word finally got through to wherever it needed to go.

Dimitri's message was that it could be an outbreak of food poisoning, and that half the town was down with it so she should go straight to Beaver Dam once she got back to Elkhorn. So she'd landed her Cessna in Elkhorn's one landing strip, picked up her Jeep, which had already been stocked with supplies and was waiting for her, courtesy of Dimitri, and had been on the road in a matter of minutes. No time to spare for a quick shower.

Flying into Beaver Dam would have been her preference. She was, after all, a licensed pilot. But Beaver Dam didn't have a clear landing area anywhere in the vicinity. So going by Jeep had been the alternative, albeit a dreary one right now since she was tired and on top of that the forecast was for snow.

Looking up at the sky again, Alek sighed. "I'd rather be home," she murmured. All cozy and warm in front of her own fireplace. "Not today, anyway. Which gives you one more night, Dimitri, before I meet your deep, dark secret." A woman! A quick phone call home from Juneau, a female voice she hadn't heard long enough to recognize, Dimitri sounding rather flustered when he'd come on the line. No wonder he'd been so keen to get rid of her for two weeks. "You're full of surprises lately, a mystery woman and a new doctor. All I can say is that I hope your choice in women is better than your choice in medical partners." It had to be, although she couldn't figure out who the woman might be. Maybe Irena from over in Gold Rush? Or Katerina Shelikov, who came up from Nome to visit her granddaughter every now and then? She'd noticed both of them having a little flirt with Dimitri from time to time. Although, to be honest, she hadn't thought he'd noticed. Apparently he had.

Smiling fondly over the man who'd been her father more years than her own father had, Alek was glad he was finally finding some happiness in his life—something outside his work. Widowed for a decade now, it was time for him to move on with someone new and Alek couldn't wait to meet her. If she made Dimitri happy, she would make Alek happy, too.

"And we'll discuss the Michael Morse situation as soon as I get back," she muttered, taking another look at the early October sky. They were still far enough south that the worst of winter hadn't quite caught up with them yet, but it was well on its way in, with the occasional heavy snow or storm. She always looked forward to that change of season—trading in the Jeep on short hops for her dogsled. Mushing was just about the only thing she did for pleasure, and she wished she had her dogs with her right now. "They would have detoured right around you, Michael," she said. "Wouldn't have even slowed down. Of course, having you there to help me won't be all that bad, will it? Perhaps I'll take a short nap and let you tend to all the diagnostic preliminaries once we arrive."

She laughed at the thought of it. The preliminaries of diagnosing food poisoning were not one of the more glamorous aspects of medicine.

"Nasty business, but someone has to do it, don't they, Michael? And around here, big medical names like yours don't get special privileges."

Glancing in her rearview mirror to make sure he was keeping up, Alek suddenly hoped he *was* on her tail. "Don't know why you chose Elkhorn, Dr. Morse, but, since you did, there's no reason not to put you to work until I can convince Dimitri to find someone else. Pity, because the bears would have enjoyed you. They're particularly fond of pompous city boys this time of the year."

Ten minutes later, Alek slowed down at a fork in the road long enough for Michael to catch up to her, then took the left option, which was little more than a footpath used by the trappers, and proceeded at a much slower speed over the snow. Barely wide enough for one vehicle, it wasn't the main road into the village, but it would shave off another twenty minutes of driving and would lead straight into Beaver Dam, a Yup'ik village consisting of craftsmen, trappers and a few fishermen who seasonally ventured out to the Chukchi Sea.

It was such a nice little village—quite peaceful and pleasant—and the people here were wonderful. She smiled, thinking about all the many forms of payment she'd received from the villagers of Beaver Dam. Local baskets, beads, dolls, parkas… One of the tourist stores in Nome sold everything paid to her and the proceeds went to the clinic, which turned out to be a nice arrangement for everyone, since the villagers would not take charity of any kind. Just like Dimitri, who operated a free clinic. Lucky for everyone that Alaskan craft had a wide appeal, especially in the lower forty-eight states, and it kept the clinic in medicine and other supplies quite nicely.

Five minutes on the little logging trail and Beaver Dam seemed to rise up out of nowhere. A plain town, consisting of one long drive-through, with a few houses scattered about, it was a village of about one hundred people, all living in neat little wooden houses. There was no ornamentation, no real road other than the dirt, which turned to mud, which turned to slush, snow or ice at this time of the year. No sidewalks. No streetlamps, although the villagers did light their front windows at sundown, which always gave the town a nice, cheery, welcoming feel.

She hadn't been here for a while because most

of the time, when there was need of a doctor, the villagers came to the clinic in Elkhorn. It was centrally located in an area between a dozen other villages, none more than a two-hour drive away. Nome, the largest city on the Seward Peninsula, was quite a bit further south from here, a good six-hour drive if the road conditions were right, and it was the next available modern source for medical care—although there were traditional healers in many of the villages. This made Dimitri's clinic vital to the well-being of the entire area since, in spite of the remote village locations, the majority of people preferred modern medicine to the older traditional ways.

Alek parked her Jeep in front of Dinook Duvak's cabin, where she would most likely spend the night, hopped out and glanced back to see if he was coming up the road. Which he was. She smiled, thinking about all the trouble the city boy could get himself into out here. He might teach wilderness medicine, might even be the best at it, but practicing what he taught was another thing, and she was going to get to see, firsthand, if his practical skills were as good as his academic verbiage.

Of course, Michael Morse didn't have to come all the way out here to find trouble. *Or be trouble.* He was quite handy at that everywhere he went—something Alek wasn't about to forget. How many nights' sleep had she lost over him? Too many! First she'd harbored a brief thought that he and she might even… But that was stupid. She'd known better. And he'd proved her right. So maybe the biggest lesson she'd learned in wilderness school was why *not* to become involved. It always hurt too much, and in the end, you always ended up hurting alone. Certainly, he'd hurt her in ways she'd never thought possible and they hadn't even been involved. "Nausea, loss of appetite, abdominal cramps, low-grade fever, malaise, diarrhea," she shouted at him before he was even out of his Jeep.

"What?" he shouted back.

"The symptoms, Doctor. I've listed the symptoms. You're the wilderness medicine expert, so you tell me what they add up to." Although she knew it was food poisoning of some sort, maybe he had a better perspective on it. As much as she detested the man, she did respect his knowledge.

"I hope they add up to a tank of gasoline," he muttered, stepping out of the Jeep. "Because that's the only reason I'm here. Not to tell you that your symptoms add up to a good case of food poisoning, which you already know, since apparently you're a medic of some sort."

A medic of some sort? If she had time for another good round of anger, that would have been the start of it, but she didn't. "You'll get your gas," she snapped. "After we get the situation settled down here."

"And you're imposing me into that situation why?"

"Because I know all about you, and you've never been shy about telling people that you're the best. I have fifty sick people here who need the best, and since by your own admission that's you…"

"Like I said, food poisoning. Maybe some kind of small-bowel overgrowth syndrome. Or another, less common enteric parasite such as *Strongyloides stercoalis* or *Trichuris trichiura*. Could be something as simple as *G. lamblia, E. histolytica* or *Costridium difficile*. It might even be a lactase deficiency induced by a small-bowel pathogen. Or maybe they simply shared contaminated moose meat. So, now that you know everything I know, do I get my gasoline?"

For a second she was amazed by how quickly it all came to him. She'd really forgotten how brilliant he was. Taunting him about it and actually hearing it in his diagnosis were two different things, and if it weren't for the fact that Michael Morse was a despicable man, she might have gushed a bit. But he was, so she wouldn't. Still, he deserved his due. He'd perfected what she practiced. And just because she'd had so many other impressions of him from the first time they'd met, that didn't lessen the fact that Michael Morse was the best of the best when it came to this kind of medicine. She probably owed him a thank-you, except she didn't have the time for it, neither did she have an inclination to be nice, because she didn't like him.

So the due he was owed wasn't going to come from her. "Grab your medical bag, Doctor. We've got fifty patients to see before the storm hits. Half the village, to be exact. If we're lucky we'll be halfway to Elkhorn before it does. And if not?" She shrugged as she grabbed her medical bag out of the back of her

Jeep and tossed a rucksack full of medicine over to him. "We might be here for days." That was a bit of an exaggeration this early in the season, but the panicked look on his face was worth the lie.

"And you're under the impression I came here to treat diarrhea?" he asked.

"I'm under the impression that you're able, and that you're here. I'm also under the impression that if you don't, and I simply take a notion to stay here for a while, you'll have to find your own way out." She dished him a sarcastic smile with that slice of exaggeration. "So grab your medical bag. We have a long evening ahead of us."

"Didn't bring it with me."

Alek blinked her surprise. "And you're supposed to do what without your medical bag?"

"Nothing. I'm supposed to do nothing except go to Elkhorn."

So he was arrogant *and* a slacker. Arrogant she remembered quite vividly. But being a slacker… "You are *the* Michael Morse who teaches wilderness medicine, aren't you? The one who holds the certification seminars and stresses being prepared *all the time* for any emergency?" As if he could be anyone else. His brown hair was a bit shorter now, still with a little curl wanting to pop out, and he had a few wrinkles around his green eyes, but it was him. *Like she could ever forget.*

A flash of irritation crossed his face. "My credentials have nothing to do with this. I'm only here to find—"

"Fine," she interrupted, her own impatience level rising above his. "Play this out however you like, but we're going to make house calls now. You take the north side of the road, I'll take the south. We'll see what we've got first, then figure out how we'll deal with it once we know for sure."

Without another word, Alek marched straight to the first house on her side of the road and knocked on the door to inquire if anyone inside was sick. As the elderly man inside pushed open the screen door to invite her in, she turned back only to find Michael standing in the road, much the way she'd found him the first time. Standing, staring. "Don't know why you hired him, Dimitri," she muttered as she stepped into the cozy parlor. More than that, she was beginning to wonder if he was all academic in his medical knowledge and no skill, because right now she sure wasn't seeing a speck of skill in a man who was touted to be the best. "The best?" she muttered under her breath as she put on her best doctor smile for the room full of villagers all waiting to see her.

"Beaver," Michael said, meeting Alek in the middle of the road thirty minutes later. He'd been waiting there ten minutes already. She'd seen him as she'd examined Maisye Strong, and had purposely delayed going outside. "Simple case of beaver poisoning. They were having a Founder's Day celebration, Ben Smiling made his world-famous beaver stew and the rest, as they say, is history. Tainted meat, although in beaver it can be a little tricky because it can come back on them for a while."

Alek shook her head, not sure what offended her more—the fact that he'd made the diagnosis in less than half an hour when she'd barely had time to see three patients, or the fact that he was just plain cocky about it. "And you've done what to validate your results, Doctor?"

"Besides asking Ben's wife? I asked his neighbor, who also ate the stew, as well as asking a woman named Dinook Duvak, who's the local doctor of sorts."

"I know Dinook," Alek snapped.

"Well, Dinook confirmed it, too, but she says she's been feeling a bit poorly herself and hasn't come up with a proper remedy." Michael gave her a lazy grin. "So now that I know who *they* are here, and what's ailing them, would you mind telling me who *you* are and why you dragged me out here to cure a case of food poisoning?"

"I'm Dr. Aleksandra Sokolov." She waited for a response of some sort from him, and blinked her astonishment when none came. Not even a shadow of recognition. "Sokolov." He was so…so brilliant, as much as she hated admitting that. So in all that brilliance, was he pretending he didn't remember her? Or did he really not remember the person who was, in his opinion, the worst doctor in the world? "I'm Dr. Aleksandra Sokolov," she repeated stiffly, still watching for a hint of recognition. There was none. She couldn't believe it, after what he'd done to her three years ago. Of course, impugning a reputation might have been an everyday thing for him because he'd been so good at it. But that had been the first, and only, time for her, and while his words might have been only in passing, they dug deep. They even made her question her abilities for a time, until she realized just what an ass he was. Nice one minute, then rude. Patient, then jumping out of his skin with restlessness. Petulant, docile…all over the place, unhinged and so composed. And so damned intelligent it made her angry just thinking about someone like him having such a phenomenal gift.

"Well, Dr. Sokolov, under different circumstances I'd say it was nice meeting you, but the only thing I really want to say is find me the gasoline you promised so I can get the hell out of here." He glanced up at the sky, frowning. "The sooner, the better."

Following his lead, Alek glanced up at the sky. She frowned, too, but not because of the sky. It was what the sky implied—that she was about to be snowed in with him. Traveling during the storm was too risky. White-out conditions added to winds so strong they could set her Jeep to spinning in circles again, plus the fact that she hated being out during a storm, were all the precipitating factors she needed for the decision to stay the night and see what morning would bring, other than snow. Snow, and Michael Morse, unfortunately. "You're not going anywhere," she said, as the first flakes started to flutter. "Too late. We're here for the night. And if we're lucky, it'll be only one night."

CHAPTER THREE

"MY GRANDSON has gone to Anchorage to work," Dinook Duvak said, as she opened the door to the tiny wooden house that sat next door to hers. It was cozy and clean, one tiny, square room with all the bare essentials. A propane stove along with a small, handcrafted table and two chairs tucked into one corner designated the kitchen. An empty desk where Dinook's grandson had apparently kept computer equipment sat in another corner. A curtained-off dressing room and makeshift bathroom occupied the third corner. Finally, in the fourth, was the bed—thankfully a single.

Standing in the center of the room was a large, wood-burning stove, with its black stovepipe jutting straight up through the ceiling. It was typical of the old Yup'ik style, where everything in the home centered around the heat source, and the living spaces were kept small to better maintain the heat. Structures weren't built that way so much now, especially in the cities, where regular furnaces and boilers were used to generate heat, but it wasn't uncommon to find the villagers in remote areas such as Beaver Dam still adhering to tradition. It was simply a more efficient way for them.

And this efficient cabin was so cramped, Alek realized that being up close and personal with Michael was going to be the order of her evening and night with him. Immediately, she felt the walls closing in around her—not from claustrophobia, but from the thought of being confined with him in that diminutive space. Too close a proximity… She could almost feel the dearth of oxygen in the snug quarters starting to choke her.

"Are you feeling poorly, too, Doctor?" Dinook asked, as she scurried to stack clean sheets on the end of the bed. "Should I have the other doctor come in to take a look at you?"

"I'm a little tired. Dimitri sent me up here before I had a chance to rest, but I'm fine, thank you. And I don't need the other doctor." Fine about everything except being here with Michael. "And how about you?"

"Better. I didn't eat much of the stew this year." She wrinkled her nose. "Between you and me, I never did have much of a taste for beaver. I eat it to be polite, but I don't go after it the way some of the others do."

Alek laughed. "Which is a good thing for you this year. So, can I give you something for the nausea?"

Dinook shook her head. "That nice doctor already did before I came in. He has such a pleasant smile, don't you know. And kind eyes. Is he working with you now?"

"No, he's not working with me," Alek said. In her mind he wasn't, although Dimitri might have something different to say about it. "I found him down at the four-way, just standing in the middle of the road. He was lost and he followed me here."

"Funny how those things happen, isn't it? I found my Kobalook standing off the side of the road like that, too. Only I was the one lost, not him. Trying to find my way from Piruiak to Nome, and along he comes in his truck." She chuckled. "I never did make it to Nome that day.

I really wanted to go to the mercantile for some fabric, but I went and got married instead."

"The day you met him?"

She nodded. "He needed a wife, he was handsome, and he told me he had a nice trap line set out so I knew he was a good provider."

And that's all there had been to it. No fuss, no muss, they were married and still happy all these years later. All because she'd been standing on the right road in the right place at the right time.

Alek thought about Michael standing in the middle of the four-way, then shook her head. Wrong road, wrong place, wrong time and definitely the wrong man. Easier that way, no matter who it was, actually. "That worked out brilliantly for you, but the only thing I intend on doing with Dr. Morse is—"

"Go on," Michael said, stepping into the room. "I'd like to know what you intend on doing with me so I can be prepared."

Alek shot him a clipped smile. "Ignoring you. That's all I intend on doing." What she should have done three years ago.

Dinook reached out and gave Alek an affectionate pat on the arm. "Just like I tried ignoring my Kobalook for the first ten minutes." She turned to Michael with a wide, gracious smile. "You can stay in this house as long as you need to. The both of you. And if you like sweet rolls, Dr. Morse—"

"Michael," he interrupted. "Call me Michael. All my friends do."

Dinook's eyes lit up. "And if you like sweet rolls, Michael, I'll be glad to fix them for you tomorrow morning."

"I love sweet rolls," he said in absolute sincerity. "But, please, don't trouble yourself on my account. Normally, I grab a cup of coffee or tea, and I'm good for hours."

"No trouble, Michael. A young man such as yourself needs more than coffee or tea to start his day." She glanced at Alek and gave her a deliberate, and obvious, wink. "Much more, like my Kobalook did, and still does."

Alek plastered a tight smile on her face through the interchange, and didn't even blink when Dinook trotted from the cabin without even asking if she, too, liked sweet rolls. "How do you do that?" she snapped, once the older woman had shut the door behind her. "You're here all of one minute and she's already waiting on you."

He shrugged. "I smiled. Works wonders, you know. You ought to try it some time. It might come as a pleasant change from your normal…well, whatever it is you call that expression you're wearing."

"It's called *I'm already getting tired of your smile, Doctor*." Alek tossed her backpack on the bed then took her proprietorial position next to it. "And don't even think about trying to coerce me out of the bed, which I'm sure you could, and would, try to do, because I won't be coerced by you. Not like the others."

"Pity. It might have been fun trying."

"Save it for someone who gives a damn, Doctor, because I don't. I'm here to do my job, and that's all I do. I don't have time for anything else, including playing your games. Or even being a spectator to them."

Michael turned to the door on his way back out to the street, then, on second thought, turned back to face her. "You're a beautiful woman, Alek, and I normally remember beautiful woman. In fact, I always remember beautiful women, and for some reason you think I should remember you. But I'm beginning to understand why I don't."

"And what's that supposed to mean?" she snarled.

"It means if you want sweet rolls, you've got to act like you deserve them. And so far, since we've met, you don't act like you deserve them." He tweaked her under the chin the way one would tweak a favorite dog, then strolled over to the kitchen area to scrounge for a box of matches.

"Like you deserve that parka someone gave you?"

"It bothers you?"

"You're what bothers me. Not the parka, not the sweet rolls." Although it did bother her that he'd ingratiated himself in mere minutes when she still questioned her own level of acceptance in the villages. They invited her in because they loved Dimitri, but how they felt about her, well, it certainly wasn't what they already felt for Michael. "Not those boots," she said, pointing to the nice pair he had on instead of the white athletic shoes he'd started with. "Give me those matches," she grumbled, swiping them out of his hand.

"Want some firewood?" he asked.

"If I want firewood, I'll get firewood." She trudged over to the log pile next to the stove, grabbed up three sizeable pieces of wood and shoved them in through the woodstove door, then set about the task of starting the fire as he stood back, watching. First two strikes didn't take, and as she was about to go for a third, she heard him step up behind her. "Are you sure I can't do that?" he asked, still keeping a reasonable distance between them.

"You diagnose better, you treat better, so why not start a fire better?" With that, she stood up and handed him the matches. "Suit yourself. Start the damned fire and I'll go out to medicate patients."

"You didn't happen to eat any of Ben's stew, did you?" he asked quite seriously as he tossed a match into the wood pile and the tinder sparked instantly. "Because everybody outside was telling me what a nice doctor you are, and what they're saying certainly isn't what I'm seeing."

"And what is it you think you're seeing, Doctor?" she hissed.

"What I'm seeing is somebody who's really

angry with me over something I didn't do, or don't recall doing."

"Well, score one for the teacher. Oh, excuse me. Isn't it the teacher who usually scores one against the student?"

He raised his eyebrows for a second and stared at her, then, without uttering a word, Michael walked straight over to Alek, pulled off her big fur hat and took a good, hard look at her. "So are you going to make me keep guessing, or come right out and tell me—give me a list of my offenses or your grievances? Or both? Because I'm not a mind-reader, Doctor. I have a great many other talents, but that's not one of them, I'm sorry to say, because right now it would come in handy."

"Go to hell," Alek snapped, backing away from him.

"Being locked up in this room with you all night, something tells me that is going to be hell. Oh, and before this lovely conversation of ours erodes to the point where we don't communicate at all, we need to get some mertroindazole to these people. I'm treating the nausea with Compazine right now—I found a little stash of it in your bag—but after talking with several of the locals I'm thinking that because of the length of time it took for them to get sick—we're right at the ten-day point—the specific form of food poisoning is most likely Giardia, which we won't know without testing, and we can't test out here. So, unless you object, that's where we start— treat it like it's Giardia, use mertroindazole or a nitrofuran derivative. And three of the villagers are pregnant, so…"

Alek shook her head impatiently. Sure, she'd wanted him here to help her work. But why did he have to be so impressive about it? Although she would never admit it to him, she was impressed. "So no treatment. I know what to do here, Doctor. I'm certified. Got a diploma from medical school. One from your class, too. Remember?"

"Actually, no, I don't. But I'll take your word for it."

Alek snatched her hat away from him and headed to the front door. "I have furazolidone in the Jeep," she said abruptly.

"Need help?"

"There are a great many things in this world I need, but your help isn't one of them."

"I sure hope this isn't your typical bedside manner," he said, cutting her off, "because if it is, I'm not sure I would have certified you. Wilderness medicine takes patience and an unwavering temperament, and you're wavering, Doctor. Wavering all over the place." He gave her a broad grin. "It's a cute waver, I'll admit, but a little off the roost for most people since, in my experience, they prefer their doctors to be pleasant. And that scowl you've been giving me ever since you tried running me down on the road isn't very pleasant."

"First off, you haven't seen my bedside manner," she snarled. "And second, I'll be sending you a bill for the dent to my front bumper—damage that was incurred because I *didn't* run you down."

"Something tells me that we're not getting along so brilliantly," he teased.

"Well, finally we agree on something, don't we?" She pointed to the spot on the floor next to the old computer desk in the opposite corner of the room. "Your side of the room, Doctor, and I'd thank you to stay as far away from me as possible."

"Trust me, when I settle in, I'll be settling in somewhere much closer to a warm spot. And you, Alek Sokolov, are anything but warm."

He watched her stomp down the wooden steps to the street, then disappear round the corner before he shrugged out of his new parka and boots. By most standards, he hadn't paid too much for them, and if he was going to be stranded here overnight, which it looked like was going to be the case, the clothing he'd brought with him wouldn't be of much use. Of course, he'd expected to be in and out of Elkhorn by now, staying in a nice, warm hotel much further out and, with his mother, awaiting a ride from a bush pilot back to Anchorage, then on to Seattle. Instead, he was stranded wherever the hell Beaver Dam was—he'd checked and it wasn't on the map—in a box of a room, with a stark, raving madwoman. A *cute*, stark, raving madwoman, though. One that intrigued him, and scared the hell out of him. In a cute way.

So she'd been in one of his classes. Made sense, but there were some awfully muzzy days in his past. Too much work, too much of a struggle to be upwardly mobile, too much…well, too much of everything else.

And no Alek Sokolov that he could recall. Or didn't want to recall, yet somehow thought he should. Although he hadn't seen enough of her yet to know for sure, he was guessing that if what was underneath all the bulky winter dressing was as good as the little he'd seen so far, she was someone no sane man would ever forget. So much fire and determination, a regular little ball of clash and conflict, and so spunky.

Damn, he wanted to remember her. Something was tugging at him, but it clearly wasn't coming through. And the frustrating thing was that she definitely remembered him. Considering the way he'd been, he shuddered to think why. "She's on the list of my offenses somewhere," he muttered, cringing at the thought. It was such a long list he'd have to pull out the reading specs to have a go at it.

"But you are cute," he said, bending to fan the growing flames. "Cute as hell, and mad as hell. Pity they don't go well together." The fire settled easily and, off and on, he wondered if he should go help her even though she'd made it pretty clear she was a solo act. His inclination was to do so, but he wasn't kidding himself about this. If he did interfere, she'd have his head, and he doubted she'd have enough compassion toward him to serve it up on even the most meager of platters. And since he did have to be cooped up with her… "So let her do it by herself," he muttered, looking out the front window at the snow. It was picking up—more wind, more of it coming down. Not a ferocious storm like he would have expected this far north, but a noticeable one.

Still, she was out in it alone. "She's wearing boots, she has a parka…" All good arguments, except there were fifty sick people out there, give or take the handful he'd already seen, all waiting for her to trudge about to find them. And even with all her fire and determination, there was no way she could get all that done alone no matter what kind of huffing and puffing she was putting on to keep him away from her. She needed help. More than that, he needed to help.

"Damn it anyway, Alek," he muttered, stepping back into his boots and grabbing up his own parka on the way out the door. "Why couldn't I have met someone on the road who owned a gas station instead of an overworked, overly angry physician who hates me and who's too stubborn for her own good?"

The doctor in him prevailed, as was always the case, and Michael slogged back out into the cold and caught up with Alek halfway to the end of town. "So what do you want me to do?" he asked, falling into step for her.

"Who said I wanted you to do anything? I'm perfectly fine attending to this on my own, wretched doctor that I am."

"The only thing wretched is your attitude, so give me a break, here. Okay? It's cold, it's snowing, I'd rather be on a beach soaking up the sun instead of flicking ice crystals off my eyelashes. But the people here need help, and while you can do it alone I can speed it up for you, cut the time in half. So let's zip to the end of the argument now, skip all the stuff that comes between the start, where you hate me, and the finish, where you still hate me, and go straight to the place where you tell me what you want me to do and I go do it."

"It's my job, Doctor, and I'll do it just fine by

myself. Always have, always will. Isn't that what you taught in your class, that in many instances we'll be the only help available? There will be no one else around to help with the work? Well, consider yourself no one."

Her voice was colder than the near subarctic winds blowing down on them. Another degree or two lower and it would snap in two like a brittle icicle, and if she had her way about it, the sharp, pointed end would pierce his heart on its fall to the ground.

"Look, Dr. Sokolov. You're the one who got out of her Jeep yelling at me about the symptoms these people were experiencing and ordering me to go out and look for patients. If memory serves, all I ever wanted was a tank of gas and directions to Elkhorn, but this is what I got and I'm trying to make the best of it. Or I would if you'd let me."

"And you found those patients, didn't you? Found them and diagnosed them. I appreciate that, Doctor. I really do, but the rest is routine follow-up which I'm quite capable of handling on my own."

"You were quite capable of handling the initial assessments on your own, too, but you didn't. In fact, you seemed to like ordering me about, so what did I do to make you even more angry than you already were? Am I paying for a sin from my past, or one of my present?"

"What you're paying for, Doctor, is that I don't like you. Okay? I really don't like you. I took your classes and you're a brilliant instructor. Probably the best in wilderness medicine. But that's as far as it goes with me. I don't like you, I don't want you here, and I'll be damned if I'm going to work side by side with you now, or in the future."

"Trust me, I don't want to be here as much as you don't want me here, and I'll be more than happy to get out of here and get back to someplace where sanity prevails. Because this is insane, lady. *You're* insane. But I'm stuck here until after the storm passes, and until someone points me in the direction of a tank of gas, I'm going to make the best of it, which includes a little medical duty, whether or not you like it. So get off your high horse and let me help." He grabbed the canvas bag of medications out of her hand and pulled out half of them. "And don't get the idea that I'm doing this for you because I'm not."

"Fine," she snapped. "Suit yourself. Doctor away, but stay out of my way when you're doing it." A gust of frigid wind caught her, blowing her forward, straight into his chest.

"You okay?" he asked, grabbing hold of her, then holding on until she was steady on her feet again. Even through all the bulk, she felt good in his arms. He expected rigid, and something colder than the temperature, but for a second he felt heat…her heat, and his own heat mingling with it. A heat that caught him a little off guard.

She shrugged out of his grip and straightened her parka before he could put any sense to that little jolt he'd felt, then had the audacity to straight-arm him when he took a step forward. Her palm to his chest, she looked at him, frowning, of course, and said, "I'm always okay, Doctor. *Always*. Now, since you insist on working, you go take the north side of the street, and I'll take the south."

"How about we save steps and you take the east end of the street, while I take the west, and maybe we'll get this done before the snow is up to our knees."

"You know, I'd rather you were on the beach,

too, soaking up the sun, and if I had the means, I'd buy you a ticket right now to send you there." Without another word, she spun around and headed directly to the west end of the village.

"I said I'd take the west end," he called after her.

"I know you did," she called back. "Which is why I will."

"Sure wish I remembered you," he muttered as he made his way through the fast-accumulating snow to the far east end of Beaver Dam, which by any measurable standards was only three city blocks away. Because somewhere deep down under all that bad mood and animal fur was someone who had certainly captured his interest, if not, under other circumstances, his fancy.

Alek wasn't like the women who usually wandered in and out of his life. They were all casual and surface, a nice week or two and he was tired of them. A hell of a bad pattern, he knew. But that's the way it used to be for him. That, and other addled habits. Now it was all work. There was no reason for anything more at this point in his life. At least, not until he was sure his life was unshakable. And Alek…she was definitely a shakable force.

This Aleksandra Sokolov…well, he didn't know what to make of her. In that bluster of an attitude that swirled around her like a storm cloud, he saw a pure passion that absolutely enthralled him. And maybe he envied it just a little. Yes, he liked his work, but when he'd returned to it, the passion hadn't come back, not like it had been before. And now, just a few hours in the wilderness had made him realize what kind of work he longed for. At his stage in the game, though, it was too late to make a course change.

Perhaps that's what attracted him to Alek. She had the game he wanted. Out here in the middle of a snowstorm, delivering nausea medicine to a pack of people who'd been poisoned by bad beaver stew, she still had a real passion for it. As angry as she was at him, it still shone through, and he wanted some of that for himself. For a second or two he'd even fancied himself working side by side with her. He chuckled. "With her in a better mood," he said, even as he tried to shake the notion from his head. He stood a better chance of survival with the bears in these parts than he did with Alek.

"But you are an interesting woman,

Aleksandra," he conceded as he trudged up to the first door and knocked. "Very interesting, indeed." So was there anybody significant in her life? Husband, lover, casual friend? Sparring partner?

With her rather tempestuous attitude, he doubted even a sparring partner would be all that safe. For sure, he was not.

And for some chaotic reason he couldn't even begin to fathom, he liked that.

CHAPTER FOUR

DEAR God, she was tired. Exhausted. Frozen.
And, above all, frustrated! What was all that
about, anyway? Falling into his arms and coming
so close to enjoying it? "You're smarter than
that," she said, as she tossed her Cossack cap on
a wooden peg, then dropped her parka on the
floor, too tired to bend over and pick it up. Not
only was she smarter than that, she knew better,
too. Those had been Michael Morse's arms she'd
felt wrapped around her for a moment after all.
And she knew what he was about. Yet even
though he'd only meant to steady her, a little
spark of electricity had nipped straight through
her. One little touch and she was going mushy
in the head over it.

Even through her parka and red plaid flannels,
there had been that jolt. "Fatigue," she
reasoned, looking back out to the street to see

if she could catch sight of him. She couldn't. Fatigue—and frustration. Because she didn't want to work with Michael. But she was already planning ways to avoid him if that became the case—different work hours for a start, more time in the field for another. She chuckled. A line drawn down the clinic hallway—her side, his side. Pity him if he stepped one toe over it! Pity him if he even came close to it.

Michael Morse at Dimitri's clinic. She still couldn't get used to the idea. They did need three doctors at the clinic. Need was up, and, as vibrant and energetic as Dimitri was right now, there was the future to think about, and at his age he did deserve a slower pace. Inevitably, it would happen, and he knew it. Which was why he'd recruited a third doctor. So as much as she wanted to be difficult about Michael, she wasn't going to be. Sure, she'd make a strong suggestion to find someone else, maybe even bribe Dimitri with a good *buzhenina* to get rid of Michael, but in the end she would abide by his decision. It was his clinic, his choice. Also, Michael wouldn't stay long. There was nothing to keep him here, and once the fascination of the wilds was over, he'd toddle on back to civilization.

She was sure of that!

Sighing, Alek peeled off the double pair of thermal socks she wore inside her boots and wiggled her chilly toes to make sure none of them had frozen solid and fallen off. Then she moved in a little closer to the fire and held out her hands, rubbing them together to absorb some of the warmth. Four hours of trudging up and down the street in the snow, handing out medicine and explaining its use, and now she was ready to hibernate for a while. "Hibernate alone," she said, glancing over to his corner of the room.

She really wanted to keep Michael Morse totally out of her mind, if only for the rest of the evening, but the harder she tried the more adamantly he stayed right there, taunting her. That warm smile of his, those twinkling eyes… Okay, so she would concede that he was gorgeous. He was! What of it? She'd known that from the first time she'd seen him in Seattle, when he'd strutted his way across the stage in the lecture hall like he had been the prince entering a grand ballroom.

By reputation, he should have been much

older, possibly wizened, surely bent. Long, white, bookish beard, naturally. "It would have made things easier," she said with a sigh. However, had it been a concert hall and Dr. Michael Morse a rock star, the women there would have been throwing panties and room keys at him.

They, including her, unfortunately. She hadn't been impervious. Like it or not, she'd tried for his attention as much as the rest of them had—only not quite so obviously. But she'd known more about wilderness medicine than the others since she'd lived the life he'd been teaching. Consequently, she'd always had her hand in the air. And the need hadn't been to show off her knowledge.

"So you're a stunner, but that has nothing to do with offsetting that fact that you're also a jerk." A jerk who'd come so close to distracting her. Thank heavens common sense had prevailed then, as it would now. And in the future. Because grooming herself to take over Dimitri's entire medical practice was her priority. As was Dimitri.

Dear Dimitri. He and Olga had raised her from the age of seven after her own father had been killed on an ice cutter, leaving her abandoned, since her mother had gone to find better opportunities in a warmer climate and had never come back. As a foster child of the Romonovs, her life had been good. Dimitri had loved her, Olga had tolerated her. And she'd enjoyed working with Dimitri almost from the first moment she'd gone to live with them—sweeping his clinic floors, answering his office phone, filing his medical charts and restocking his medical supplies. So many things to make her feel important and loved—something she hadn't felt even with her parents…a father who had rarely been home, a mother who had rarely been happy.

She'd developed a passion for all things medical because of Dimitri. Passion, direction and, ultimately, the support to get her where she wanted to be, which was at Dimitri's side in the clinic as his partner. He'd been such a dear when she'd been young, always telling her about how the two of them would cure people together. He'd said they would fly away to a remote village together to perform a surgery or deliver a baby. All of this had been so much security for a lost little girl who'd desperately needed love and a place to belong. Olga, however, had been staunch and impersonal. She hadn't been a warm woman and she'd had no affinity for children, especially one like Alek who'd just appeared in her home one day, clinging to Dimitri's hand and holding on to her bag full of clothes, hoping for a new home and family. Olga had been fair to Alek. Not kind and loving, like Dimitri. But fair. And for a young child who hadn't understood why her mother hadn't returned for her, or why her father had died, Dimitri, not Olga, had become her safety. Curling up on Dimitri's lap at night while he'd read her bedtime stories, and tugging on his beard as her own secret signal to him that she wanted to give him a kiss…she had felt safe with him, and never so alone as being alone in Alaska could feel.

But she loved Alaska, too. In a way, it held its own safety for her. The snow in the winter and the beautiful green wildlands in the warmer months…it was such an exciting diversity, and she adored the splendid isolation of it all. This was the only place she wanted to be, the only place she ever would be—her heart and home. "But I wouldn't mind if the snow was a little warmer," she said, chuckling, as she leaned forward to rub her chilly feet. A nice man to rub her chilly feet would be good, too. But that wasn't in her future. Not if she stayed here, which she would. At her age she was already too old to start something new, anyway. Too old and set in her ways, which Dimitri complained of all the time. But then, this part of Alaska wasn't exactly teaming with eligibles, so she could be as set as she wanted since it didn't matter. "Most of the time it doesn't…."

Shutting her eyes to enjoy the heat coming from the stove, images of a warm, sandy tropical beach popped into Alek's head. She'd never seen a real canvas cabana chair, but on this little imaginary stretch of white sand she was lounging in one, sipping something luscious and fruity. And… Great, just great! Michael was there, right next to her on the beach, stretched out in a canvas cabana chair, too, also sipping something luscious and fruity. And he looked so much better in his little black swimming trunks than he did in his big, bulky parka. *Much better.* Naturally, she looked ridiculous, being the only one on that beach wearing a parka. She could almost hear Dimitri clucking his tongue, and see him shaking his head over her little fantasy. "Too old for your young years, Alek," he always said. "Too serious, too fussy, too set in your ways." Right now he would also add, "And you can't even do justice to a good daydream."

Which was true, because even though it was her fantasy and she should be able to control it any way she liked, she simply could not take that damned parka off, as hard as she tried.

"So you're right, Dimitri. I can't even put on a good fantasy." She walked across the room once her feet were sufficiently warmed, and dropped down onto the bed. "No big deal, though. Fantasies never accomplish anything, anyway." Except, perhaps, build a dream. But she didn't allow dreams.

Settling in finally, trying to fight off the dreams and fantasies she was afraid might endeavor to creep back in, Alek concentrated on the night sounds from outside—the barking of a far-off dog team, the whistling of the wind coming down through the chimney, the rattling of the doors and shutters trying to keep the winter out, the monotonous throbbing of the generator providing electricity for the cabin.

All busy sounds—sounds of the life that bustled around Beaver Dam. But no sounds of Michael, and as much as she didn't like him, and didn't want him hanging about, she was beginning to get worried. "City boy meets a cold Alaskan night." There were any number of images that could play through that scene— Michael lying on the side of the road, or getting lost, maybe confronting a pack of wolves, or, best of all, trying frantically to pull his boots back on as he came face-to-face with an angry husband… That one did bring a bit of a smile to her face because if that husband chased him out of town she would not have to deal with him. Win-win situation. "Whatever it is, you don't stand a chance, city boy," she muttered, trying hard to fight off the urge to get up and go look for him now that she was all cozy and warm. Of course, somebody did have to save him—from the elements, from himself….

Actually, she'd half expected to find him all curled up in her bed when she'd got back, since his half of the town was far less than hers in its count of sick people. Surprisingly, she was a bit disappointed. Not disappointed that he wasn't in her bed, but that he wasn't back. She really hadn't intended to have a pleasant evening with him, a nice chat at the fireside, some lively professional debate, but she'd intended to have him someplace safe where she didn't have to worry over him. And now, as she tossed and turned in bed, she was steadily growing more concerned that maybe he really had gotten lost. "You turn the wilderness doctor loose in the wilderness and he manages to get himself disoriented. And now I've got to go out and find him." She dropped her feet over the side of the bed, wrestling with the idea of giving him one more hour. But common sense prevailed. "If he injures himself, I'll have to take care of him. If he gets lost, I'll have to wait around until the rescue party finds him."

Two unacceptable inconveniences, both of which forced her to her feet to begin the hunt.

By the time Alek was completely outfitted for the weather, the drift at the front of the house had piled up another half foot, so she grabbed the snow shovel that sat behind the door and started to shovel her way outside. "Not worth it," she muttered as she dug through the first patch, which came halfway up to her knees. "You're not worth it, not worth me getting cold, not worth me losing sleep," she hissed into the frigid air. "And you'd better be dead, or close to it, or, so help me, I'm going to—"

"Need some help with that?" Michael called out from somewhere in the shadows beyond the front walk.

"Where have you been?" Alek snapped, straightening up and looking around until she found him. Bundled in his parka with snow most of the way up his boots, he was trudging through the snow, clutching a package in his arms.

"Having supper with Aklanuk Mountain, then afterward another supper with Simel Malemute. Friendly people. Quite hospitable, and I couldn't turn them down when they offered."

"Supper? You were out having supper all over the village while I was stuck here worrying about—" She snapped off the rest of her words before they were out, silently scolding herself for almost saying something that would have been, undoubtedly, interpreted by him as genuine concern. Which it was not!

Stepping out of his way as he passed by her and

went inside, she followed, and gave the door a good slam shut.

He turned to face her. "You were worrying about *me*? Is that what you were going to say? Somehow I would have never expected that from you."

"Good thing, then, because I wasn't worrying about *you*. I was worrying about the patients I trusted to you. Worrying if you'd seen them as you'd said you would do."

Smiling, Michael held out a brown paper bag to her, then jiggled it when she refused to take the several necessary steps toward him to remove it from his hand. Instead, she huddled at the door, frowning. "Alahseey Malemute sent you a little gift. She said she was sorry you couldn't come to eat with us but she wanted you to have a piece of custard pie."

Alek eyed the bag longingly for a second, then looked away. "I was working, Michael. Did you happen to do any of that yourself while you were out socializing?" Alahseey made the best pies. Amazing pies. Any flavor. Prize-worthy and so scrumptious that Alek's mouth was watering thinking about the custard, since all she'd managed for supper had been some instant noodle soup she'd found in the cupboard. Yes, she'd had invitations, too, but she hadn't taken the time to stop and eat because she'd had work to finish. Besides, she wasn't as good at socializing as he was. Michael was a natural at it—she'd seen that in his classroom. He'd had a real aptitude for hobnobbing, while she'd been awkward. Rejection issues, according to Dimitri. Which was probably true, as her mother had rejected her. Whatever the reason, she rarely accepted the friendly invitations because it was easier not to. And now she wasn't about to take the pie from him as it was only his way of trying to placate her, to disarm her like he did everybody else. She wasn't about to be placated. Or disarmed!

"In between my many social engagements I did manage to medicate the people who needed it. No one's in need of being hospitalized, and I did have a talk with Ben Smiling about proper meat preparation and storage. I also looked in on someone named Dalakaduk who's recovering from a broken leg quite nicely. I upped her exercise regime by half and told her to walk more. She's being a bit sluggish about that, which puts her at risk for blood clots, so I explained the complications that could set in and convinced her to do more of her own housework now instead of having her children do it all. And she was agreeable. But I would suggest that you look in on her again in another couple of weeks to make sure she's following doctor's orders because I think she's been enjoying the life of leisure."

"Are you implying that I didn't give her good instruction?" Alek snapped.

"Actually, I know that you did. She told me exactly what you'd prescribed for her, but she also told me that it was easier not doing what she was supposed to."

"And you convinced her to get up and move about?" She snapped her fingers. "Just like that?"

Pulling off his mittens, he snapped his own fingers, only harder, for emphasis. "More like that. She's stubborn, like you. Doesn't give in easily to friendly persuasion, either."

"So what did you do?"

"Smiled when I asked. And bribed her kiddies not to wait on her so much. After that, I checked on the bunions of someone named Chug Buckner, a referral from Dalakaduk. Apparently,

Chug is her father, and he's had these outrageous bunions on his feet for—"

"Chuglak," Alek corrected. "Not Chug." A nickname was reserved for only the closest of friends, and in the local tradition a person's name was not to be taken lightly. That little bit of tradition had started well over a century ago at a time when the early settlers had been moving in and changing the names of the villagers to more understandable, pronounceable Anglicized names. Because so many of the people here still bore the tales, somewhat sadly, of what their names had once been and how they had been changed, she was always careful to be respectful. "His name is *Chuglak*."

"Chuglak, who likes to be called Chug, apparently. At least, that's what he told me when he asked me to call him Chug. Oh, and I pulled Aryeh Tillion's tooth, by the way. It was a referral from Chug, his cousin. Aryeh had a nasty little infection going on in a back molar and asked if I would do the honors of yanking it for him, so I did."

"You pulled his tooth? *With what*?" This was incredible. In the dozen times she'd seen Chuglak Buckner for his aching bunions he'd never once asked her to call him Chug. As for Aryeh Tillion's tooth, she'd been trying to pull it for months, but he'd always refused, always told her it was getting better.

"I used what I had handy. A pair of pliers and a fifth of whiskey. That's all it took, and it was quite easy, actually. Came right on out after a couple of tugs, nice and clean, root intact, Aryeh so liquored up he's still probably waiting for me to have a go at it."

"You can't do that!" she snapped, inching her way over to the fire—on the opposite side of the stove from where he was standing. "I mean, how could you just…just get him drunk and pull his tooth? There are medical boundaries, even up here, Doctor."

"Medical boundaries you forced me into when you slowed down enough to allow me to follow you all the way to Beaver Dam. And you did slow down, Alek. You can't deny that, since I've seen the way you *really* drive. So you did want me here, and that's the same as opening up those boundaries for me. As far as Aryeh was concerned, what was I supposed to do? Walk away from him when he was begging me to have a yank on his tooth?" Michael bent down to lay the bag with the pie on the floor, then he pulled off his boots, saying at the same time, "I didn't come here to work, Dr. Sokolov, but that's where you put me in spite of the way you keep squawking about it, and I'm doing a damn fine job of it under the circumstances, so get off the sour attitude, will you? Or get yourself out there and do it all by yourself. Which, actually, Annabelle Donawiak is waiting for you to do first thing tomorrow morning." Standing back up, he gave the bag with the pie a little nudge with his toe, scooting it over closer to her side of the stove. "Jeannie, her fourteen year-old daughter, is moaning around with a good case of mittelschmerz, so I told her to use an ice pack for the night and that I'd send you over in the morning to explain it."

"Mittelschmerz?" Alek shook her head incredulously. The man was superhuman. He'd had a run at every medical problem in the village, and been a smashing success at it.

"Mittelschmerz. You know, ovarian pain in mid-menstrual cycle. Lower abdomen, lasts about half a day then goes away for a month.

And, yes, before you ask, without a pelvic exam, which I wasn't equipped to do out here, I diagnosed mittelschmerz from the symptoms and history. Perfectly acceptable under the circumstances, especially since Annabelle thought it might be food poisoning. But Jeannie hadn't eaten any of the stew and after a little chat, and figuring out the dates—and I did palpate her belly—I decided mittelschmerz was as likely as anything. But I didn't prescribe anything. You'll need to get her into the stirrups and have a look before you decide what to do."

"You didn't happen to cut anybody open while you were at it, did you? Remove a gall bladder or an appendix I should know about? How about a little heart surgery or a hip replacement?"

"I shaved Chug Buckner's bunions, which, I suppose, is technically minor surgery." He pulled off his parka and slung it over a chair. "Thanks for clearing me a path home, by the way. I had a couple of offers to stay elsewhere, but I really did want to come back to the place where I was the least wanted." He gave her a huge grin. "Keeps a man like me humble, you know. Humble and in his place."

"What would you know about humility? And especially about being kept in your place?" There was nothing humble at all about Michael Morse, especially on that day he'd called her out in front of the class for being wrong about how to manage a simple cold-water trauma. He'd said, "You there, in the back row. True or false? A conscious victim suffering hypothermia due to a cold-water immersion shouldn't be required to assist in their own rescue or ambulate once they are out of the water." Which was true, because that kind of activity did increase the likelihood of ventricular fibrillation. But she'd thought he'd said that a cold-water victim *should* assist and ambulate, and so she'd answered False. Michael had immediately informed the class that the student in the back row had killed her patient. "You should never allow your patient to assist, or ambulate afterward, because that could cause them to go into V-fib and die. Which is what your patient did. He died because his inept physician didn't know the correct procedure."

"But I thought you said—" she'd started to argue.

"If you'd been listening properly, you'd know what I said," he interrupted, "then your theoretical patient wouldn't be dead. I hope you listen better to your live patients, Doctor, because if you don't, you'll be leaving quite a body count in your wake."

Her temper had flared and she would have argued the point, but he had moved on to an in-depth discussion of the topic so quickly, she had been left to slink down in her seat, take notes and hope the flush of humiliation passed quickly. When he'd ended the class for the day, he'd gotten away before she'd had a chance to chase him down and tell him what an impolite pile of moose droppings he was.

That had been abject humiliation at its worst. And to top it off, even as he'd stridden off the stage, her heart had still skipped a beat. Love, hate, or even love-hate…she didn't understand it, but it didn't matter, anyway. Class ended in another week, and she'd never have to see the jerk again. But the very next day on her way into class, he'd smiled at her as if nothing had happened, and her heart had done that same, stupid lurch as she'd taken her same seat in the back row.

"What do I know about humility?" he said, as he pulled off his boots then threw his backpack over next to the fire. "You know, Alek, you take yourself far too seriously. Life's too short to go about in a snit all the time. And it's a pity, because underneath all the grouchiness I think you might have a nice smile, if you'd ever care to use it."

"I'm not in a snit all the time, Michael. Only the time spent with you."

"Damn, I sure wish I knew what I did to make such a bad impression on you. And I'm beginning to wish you'd made the same bad impression on me so we'd at least be equal in this battle. But you've got the advantage, Alek. You know what I did and I don't." He tossed her a devilish wink. "And if I owe you an apology, I'll be more than happy to extend it just as soon as you do me the courtesy of telling me what I did to deserve so much of your wrath."

"Not wrath so much as wariness, Michael. You deserve my wariness and, trust me, I am wary."

"Wariness with a great big frown line between your eyes. And it's not becoming, because you have eyes that were meant to sparkle and shine, but in some way I don't believe they do that so much, do they? And it has nothing to do with me."

"And how is that any of your business?"

"It's not. But your attitude toward me is, and I helped myself to a little further comment."

"Look, Michael. Since we're stranded here together for the night, can't we just agree to disagree, and leave it at that? Skip the small talk, don't bother about the arguments, avoid the taunting and simply agree that we won't?"

"Except that you're the only one disagreeing here, which can't be much fun, putting yourself through something like that when you don't have to. I mean, with the way you're acting, if anyone here should be disagreeable, it's me." He drew in a deep sigh and let it out slowly. "But it's not worth it. Trust me. I learned the hard way that life's too short and there are so many more pleasurable things to do than be disagreeable."

Alek watched him walk over to the woodstove, his strides casual, then sit down cross-legged on the wooden floor in front of it. "But some people warrant disagreeable," she argued. He was so comfortable here—he fit in perfectly and naturally, and got along so well. Much better than she did, actually. And she did try, but she simply wasn't good at it the way he was. Even on her best day, which this was not. "So why are you here, Michael?" she asked, trying not to sound too curious about it, even though she was.

"Looking for gasoline. I believe that was the original reason, wasn't it? Desperate man stranded out on the lonely road, lost, low on gas. Beautiful woman comes along and spirits him away to this exotic location for a night of fun, passion and medical diagnosis in exchange for a can of gas. And, trust me, I'd prefer the gas over the fun and passion." He pulled Alahseey's pie from the bag and sat the plastic container on the floor. "Wouldn't mind a good coffee right about now, though."

"And you expect me to make it?"

"I'd like for you to join me after I make it, since with your temper I'm not sure what I'd find my cup spiked with."

"There's some instant in the cupboard," she said stiffly. "And I suppose this piece of pie is large enough for the two of us to share," she continued, more out of politeness than actually wanting to share anything with him. But a vision of the two of them with one slice of pie to share did flash through her mind. Nice, pleasant thought. Cozy, intimate… *Talk about emotions betraying common sense!*

What was all that about, anyway?

Instantly Alek looked to see if he was paying attention to her, and when she caught him smiling, she cleared her throat, straightened her shoulders and scooted further around the stove so he wouldn't see her quite so well.

"I appreciate the offer to share," he said, "even though I'm not sure it was really a genuine offer, judging from the scowl on your face now. But I've already had more than my share."

"Yes, you have, haven't you?" she said flatly, noticing that her voice was a bit wobbly. Red face, wobbly voice. Not good!

"And you're really not going to tell me what this is about, in case I need to make amends, are you?" After pouring the water from the faucet into a small tin coffeepot, Michael placed it on the stove then sat back down with her. "Can I guess, though?"

"Nothing to guess," she said, scooting away from him.

"And to think I missed being on a nice, warm beach for all this." He spread his arms in a wide, sweeping gesture. "Maui would have been good, I think. Right now I would be warm. Half-naked, too. And drinking one of those tropical drinks with lots of fruit and a paper umbrella in it. Ogling the bikinis, of course. Wouldn't be very sporting of me not to ogle them, would it?"

Alek laughed in spite of not wanting to. He tried hard to be nice. She had to give him credit. The bigger her fuss, the harder he tried to charm his way in. So maybe it was just a game for him. Or maybe he was genuinely appealing and this wasn't put on. Whatever the case, he played his end of it well, and she could see why people succumbed to him. He was easy to succumb to, and, as staunch as she was about detesting him, she was beginning to find it difficult to hold her attitude for long stretches. Especially when he was inching his way over to her, brandishing that dratted custard pie. "Ogling the bikinis I can believe," she said, trying not to relax too much, "but I don't picture you as the type who would want a paper umbrella. I think maybe one of those little plastic swords like a pirate might carry would suit you better. Skewer lots of sour fruit with it." She wrinkled her nose and laughed, in spite of herself.

"Not a sword. I like the symbolism of a paper umbrella. It means you're on holiday, doing something you wouldn't normally do. And judging from your inhospitable reaction to me, it would seem that you would think I might be inclined to the sword on a regular basis, so it absolutely has to be the paper umbrella. No exceptions."

"We do have those paper umbrellas in Alaska, you know."

"Yes, but it's not the same when they have little icicles hanging off them. And you really don't have much in the way of good bikini weather here at this time of the year, either." He scooted the pie, centimeter by centimeter, in her direction. "And gooseflesh just doesn't look all that good in a bikini, in my opinion."

This was a pleasant chat, she decided. Of course, she was still on her guard. Pleasant was one thing, but the *real* Michael Morse was something else altogether, and she couldn't forget that because she'd already experienced what came after pleasant. "Bikinis and paper umbrellas notwithstanding, why *did* you come to Alaska if you really wanted Maui?"

"To find my mother," he replied quite simply.

That hadn't been what she'd expected to hear. "She's lost?"

"In a way, I suppose. My dad died a year ago and she's only now beginning to get over the trauma of it."

"I'm so sorry," she said, instinctively laying her hand atop his and giving it a squeeze. "It takes so long to get over something like that, and I do know how difficult that can be. The little memories that pop right in when you don't expect them, the simple things reminding you, things that are always there, that you can't escape. Sights, sounds, even smells…" She stopped when she realized her hand was still on his, and that she was allowing him into a place she allowed no one. Jerking back her hand like a toddler who'd touched a hot stove, she tucked it into her pocket. "I'm sorry for your loss, and for your mother's," she whispered, staring into the fire, trying to regain her usual starched composure. "So how did she get here?"

"I suggested that she take a cruise, and she did. Of course, when I mentioned a cruise I assumed it would be to someplace tropical, or maybe to the Mediterranean. But for whatever her reason, which she didn't explain to me, she came to Alaska instead. Then somewhere along the way, and I don't really know the proper sequence of all this, she went to work for a man who managed to intrigue her, and now he's taking advantage of her while she's still so vulnerable, after forty years with my father. Probably robbing her of every penny she has, too."

"How awful," Alek gasped. Then it dawned on her that Michael was not here to work in Dimitri's clinic after all. Being on the road when he was had been a coincidence, and suddenly she felt horrible about dragging him here with his mother in danger when all he wanted was the quickest way to find her. "I'm so sorry about the way I've acted, Michael. I think I've made a terrible mistake about you." Which didn't alter the fact that she still didn't like him. But she did allow that a man like Michael Morse could have an affectionate spot for his mother.

He gave her his best casual grin, the one she was already getting used to, as he poured the hot water over the instant coffee grounds then handed her the steaming mug. "Apology accepted. So now, tell me what you're sorry for."

"I thought you were here to work. When I saw you out on the road, and realized who you were, I assumed you were the one who—"

"You assumed I'd given up wilderness teaching to do wilderness doctoring." He chuckled, shaking his head. "Believe me, if I had, you'd have scared me away."

She did deserve that comment, after all. And she wasn't even going to argue with him over it. "Well, I was wrong, and I apologize. So, send me a bill for your services, because I certainly intend on paying—"

"All I want is a tank of gasoline," he interrupted. "That's it. One tank, and a map to Elkhorn, then we'll call it even." He poured himself a cup of coffee, then took a sip. "And it hasn't been a horrible experience. Under different circumstances, I might have enjoyed it more. The people are nice, and it's always good to get practical field experience to go along with my teaching."

"But you like city life better."

He shrugged. "It's what I do, but I don't mind going out on a good rescue every now and then. Even if it's only food poisoning. It's a nice change, and if I weren't looking for my mother…"

"Who you think is in Elkhorn?" It was the largest town in these parts and she knew everyone there, but she couldn't think of a single man who would be taking advantage of a vulnerable widow. Not a single, solitary man. "And you're sure it's Elkhorn, because I know everybody there and I can't think of anybody who would do such a thing to her."

"Oh, it's Elkhorn. Through a modern invention called e-mail, I *know* she's in Elkhorn, living with some bastard called Dimitri Romonov. He's a doctor, she's a doctor… Since you're a doctor from these parts, too, do you know him?"

CHAPTER FIVE

"Do I know him?" Alek sputtered, so shocked she could barely get his name out. "You *are* joking with me, aren't you? I work with Dimitri. I work at the Romonov Clinic, and when I return, apparently I'll be working with your mother if she's the woman I think Dimitri has with him." How could it be anyone else? Doctor Morse. Just not Dr. *Michael* Morse.

"I rarely joke when it comes to my mother's goodwill being compromised. Which is what this Dimitri Romonov is doing. Taking advantage of her while she's still in mourning for my father. Trust me, it's not a joke."

This was so unreal, this accusation against Dimitri, she couldn't yet find the words to come to his defense. "Meaning what?" she snarled.

"Meaning, I'm going to contact the Alaska

medical authorities and have them look into his licensing."

"You're what?"

"The guy's running a quack clinic, but you know that if you're working for him."

"Not for him, Michael. With him. Which makes me not only an inept physician but a quack as well. I know how you define inept, so tell me how you define quack?" she snapped, fighting to hold her temper. She didn't want this to erode until she had all the ammunition she'd need for the real fight.

"Pneumonia jacket and an asafetida bag, for starters. That's quackery in any modern medical text, and my mother's getting herself involved in it."

Alek bit her lip, not sure if she wanted to laugh or yell. This was so absurd. A pneumonia jacket was a traditional cure from nearly a century ago, when there had been no real treatment for lung disease. It was a basic, heavy cotton vest placed on a patient, then every day an inch was cut away. In theory, when the vest was gone, so was the pneumonia. It worked if the patient was likely to be cured, and the simple fact was that most people did survive pneumonia. So the pneumonia jacket was looked upon as a miracle. And, yes, as a placebo. They did still use it in the clinic for certain people who adhered to the very old ways. An ancient pneumonia jacket, along with some very modern drugs.

As for the asafetida—that was a bit too gummy, and getting those Asian plants to Alaska for the purpose of curing lung spasms was a hefty challenge, especially when a prescribed pill was easier. Although she and Dimitri did like eucalyptus. Of course, Michael would consider that quackery, too.

"And you have a problem with quackery—you who pulled a tooth using whiskey as a painkiller?"

"Okay, so that wasn't orthodox. I'll admit it. But she's practicing without the benefit of the modern conveniences she's used to, which could open her up to a medical-malpractice lawsuit."

"If the people up here were inclined to sue, which they're not. And *you* treated a whole town without the benefit of the modern conveniences you're used to."

"Different circumstances. You can't construe a one-time situation to be anything like a full-time profession. Besides, he's not paying her. Not one blessed penny."

"She told you that?"

He nodded. "It's all volunteer."

"People do it all the time. Altruistic doctors do it all the time. Ever hear of Doctors Without Borders? Ever been to a free clinic in the inner city? We're not all mercenary, Michael. We don't all get a thousand dollars every time we utter a professional opinion, and maybe your mother simply decided it was time to find a new way. But there's really no point in arguing this with you, is there, since I'm an inept, quack doctor who finds it as easy to kill a patient as cure one, further proving my horrible medical judgment?"

"What the hell?" he exclaimed.

"What the hell is, you're wrong about Dimitri, and about what we do at the clinic. And I swear, if you go to Elkhorn and make trouble for him, I'll—"

"What?" he interrupted. "Threaten me with your police powers? Look, Alek, my mother spent an entire year being depressed and, God knows, I did everything to help her and couldn't. Then one day, out of the blue, I get an e-mail telling me that her whole life is changed now. An e-mail, not even a phone call. What am I supposed to think?"

"That, perhaps, her whole life is changed. Maybe she's happy again."

"Changed so much she won't talk to me, won't return calls, won't even return e-mails, except to say that all's well?"

"With your attitude, I can't say that I blame her. You make harsh judgments, Michael. Harsh and hurtful, and you don't look to see who you're hurting." She drew in a deep breath, trying to steady her nerves so this argument wouldn't degrade into something personal, since it did involve Dimitri so deeply. "Just leave them alone. Okay? Let them work out whatever it is they're doing—working, having a relationship, both—because in the end, it's none of your business."

"You can defend your Dimitri all you want, but can you tell me why my mother has drawn nearly a hundred thousand dollars out of her bank account as a check made out to him?"

Alek blinked back her astonishment. Dimitri never took charity or handouts for any reason.

Not ever. If a patient wanted to pay a bill, he accepted what he was owed, and only that. And often he didn't even accept that much. But if someone wanted to contribute more, wanted to make a contribution of any kind to the clinic, Dimitri turned it down flatly, without exception. "Do you know that for a fact, that she gave him that much money?"

Michael pulled his backpack over to him, unzipped the outside compartment and pulled out a sheet of paper. "This is what I know for a fact," he said, handing it over to Alek.

She took a quick look and sucked in a sharp breath. Yes, it was a photocopy of a check and, yes, Dimitri's name was on it as the recipient. But that didn't necessarily mean anything. It couldn't! "Which proves nothing," she said, shoving the paper back to Michael.

"It proves everything."

Alek took a firm grip on her coffee mug, willing herself not to throw it at him. "Dimitri wouldn't accept charity from anybody. And you'd better learn the facts before you make any more accusations, because walking to Elkhorn in the snow won't be pleasant, and in case you haven't figured it out by now, you're on the verge of a very long, cold walk."

Without another word Alek got up and marched over to her bed in the corner. If there had been any feasible way to get him out of this cabin right now, she would have. But by now the village was rolled up and tucked in and, barring an emergency, no one would be awake to take Michael in for the night. And as much as she despised the man, she wouldn't put him out in the cold, which was what he deserved.

"You defending Romonov still doesn't change the fact that he has a large chunk of my mother's money in his bank account. Blind loyalty is admirable, but not always wise, Alek."

"Neither are you, Michael!" she snapped.

Michael threw his hands into the air in mock surrender. "Hey, lady. All I want is gasoline. Okay? That's the only thing I've asked of you, and that's all I'm expecting from you. Granted, I've offended you in the past, and if I remembered you I might recall what I did to deserve this. Or not deserve this. But since I don't, you'd call any attempt at an apology I might make insincere or hypocritical, so I'll spare you the effort. I've done a great many things in my life for which I've offered a great many apologies, but I will never apologize for protecting my mother, and if that means involving your medical partner, so be it. I'll do what I have to do."

There were so many more things she wanted to say, but he simply wasn't worth the breath it took to continue the argument, because people like Michael Morse didn't listen, and they didn't change. To think she might have been attracted to him once astounded her. "Stay on that side of the cabin, Doctor. And I'm warning you, don't you dare say another word against Dimitri or you're going to be sleeping out in the cold." And she meant it…probably.

Plopping down on the bed, Alek turned her back to Michael and pulled the wool blanket up all the way over her shoulders. Promise or not, come morning she wasn't going to lead him to Elkhorn like the Pied Piper leading the rats. Get him his gas, give him directions, and he was on his own, because the sooner he got to Elkhorn, the sooner he would start to cause problems. And while she couldn't stop the inevitable from happening, maybe she could postpone it long enough that he might have second thoughts. Give him a good little delay here in Beaver Dam before he set off for Elkhorn. Good plan, although it probably wouldn't work.

Across the room, which was only a good ten paces away, Michael chuckled. An annoying chuckle. One that grated all the way up her spine. "What?" she snarled.

"Just trying to imagine you in bed. With that attitude, I'll bet you keep it mighty hot under the sheets on these long, cold Alaskan nights."

He'd watched her fidget for a good ten minutes now. She was itching to fight with him again—come out swinging one more time to defend her friend, Dimitri. She'd been twisting and turning and huffing out over-exaggerated sighs. "Is there something else you wanted to say to me?" he asked, knowing she had plenty on her mind. But he couldn't help provoking her. She was so cute when she was provoked. "Another fight, perhaps? Maybe an accusation? An opinion, a denial, a good round of name-calling?"

"Would you shut up?" Alek snapped, her face still turned to the wall. "I'm trying to sleep."

"And I can hear you. No wonder you're still awake. It's pretty noisy in your half of the room." But he was mildly entertained by her annoyance. Normally, women fawned over him. He wasn't sure why, and he'd never complained. His looks were okay, not great, not horrible. His personality was good enough, not flamboyant, not flat. He worked in a hospital, not a private practice, so he wasn't wealthy by a long shot. But when it came to women, he'd been lucky. Probably luckier than he deserved since not a one of them had ever struck his fancy in any way.

Of course, that was all in the past. A good year behind him now, and counting forward. Honestly, by the time he'd hit thirty, he had been tired of the life, tired of dating, tired of hooking up, tired of all the old habits. Work all day, play all night—it wore him down, especially when what he wanted wasn't there. He couldn't even define what that was. Defining what he *didn't* want was much easier. Pretty much, he didn't want anything he'd had, the things that had caused him so many problems in the end, problems that had nearly unraveled his whole life. Ambition to be more, even when he didn't know what more was, became a deadly intoxicant.

So now he went home to a cup of hot tea at night, then settled in. Boring, but safe. But that was fine. And sometimes, when the lonely hours hit, he simply worked more to overcome them.

He suspected Aleksandra Sokolov would never believe that of him. Somehow she fancied him to be the troll under the bridge, always ready to extract something from someone, and that was before she'd known he was here to fetch his mother. "When, exactly, did you take my class?"

"Three years ago, summer course."

Which did make some sense now. He cringed over the bad memory. "So maybe I do owe you an apology at that. I wasn't at my best that summer. Had some personal problems." A mild understatement. It was more like that had been the beginning of his major upheaval.

"Not at your best?" she sputtered. "Is that what you call it?"

"We all have bad times."

"We certainly do, and I'm having one of those right now. And the apology's not worth anything,

Dr. Morse. Not coming from you. So I'd thank you to shut up and let me sleep, now."

It was the fifth knock on the door and wearily, Alek concluded that whoever was outside wasn't going away. She also concluded that Michael wasn't going to answer. Resigned to losing the rest of her night's sleep, Alek rolled out of bed, took a look at Michael—who was either sleeping so soundly he hadn't heard the faint tapping or was the best faker she'd ever seen—and trudged to the door, dreading to open it to the outside elements. She didn't mind snow, didn't even hate the cold, but she loathed being called out into it in the middle of the night. It was part of the job, but there was no requirement that she should like this aspect.

"Hello, Dr. Alek," she heard a tiny voice call from outside.

Immediately she pulled open the door, to find a young girl standing there. She was bundled in a heavy parka with a wool scarf pulled up around her face, and only her worried eyes were visible. "Noora?" Noora Eyinck lived outside town, about two kilometers away. In the middle of the night, in the snow, it couldn't have been an easy walk for the waif, and already Alek was alarmed to find her here.

"Mama is sick tonight," she said, standing her ground on the threshold even as Alek stepped aside to let her in. "She doesn't want you coming, but she's got the bellyache awful and she's not breathing so well."

"How long has she had the bellyache?" Alek asked.

"Since supper. She said it will go away, and my grandma's there to help her get better. But when it comes on her she sounds like it hurts so bad."

"Do you know her?" Michael asked Alek, having woken up. "Does she have an ulcer or reflux disease?"

"Not that I know of. She gets her immunizations, makes sure her family is updated in their health care, but that's it. No medical history that I recall."

"Beaver stew," Michael said. "Delayed onset. Rare, but it can happen." He looked at the girl. "Did she eat Ben Smiling's stew?"

Noora shook her head adamantly. "We didn't go this year. Mama was tired, and Papa is away fishing."

"So I make a house call," Alek said, holding out her hand to Noora as the child stepped into the house. "Does she know you're here?" Alek asked her. She was betting Mrs. Eyinck didn't know. The Yup'ik were very close-knit and protective of their families. A child Noora's age, nine, would never be allowed out of the house to wander around on her own in the middle of the night.

"No, ma'am. My grandma was tending to her when I left. I heard you came here for everybody else that was sick like my mama is, so I thought you should come and give her some medicine, too." She walked straight over to the fire to warm her hands. "My mama says that tomorrow when she's all better, I'll have a new brother or sister to play with, which is why I came to get you. I've never had a brother or sister before, and I want her to get better so I can have one."

Alek and Michael shot each other a surprised look. "She's pregnant?" he asked, grabbing up Alek's rucksack full of medicines, then stepping into his fur boots and pulling on his parka.

Shrugging, Alek responded, "They don't always come to us for such things. Poisoned beaver stew, yes. Childbirth, no." She shrugged on her own parka, then pulled her Cossack cap over her head and tucked her hair up under it. "And under the bulky clothes they wear, sometimes I can look straight at them and not even realize they're nine months along and on the verge of giving birth." She yanked her rucksack away from him, then snatched up her medical bag. "So can you drive in the snow, city boy?"

"We have snow in Seattle," he said. "It's not only an Alaskan commodity."

She tossed him the keys to her Jeep. "Then prove yourself, Doctor. Just watch out for the bears. They don't take too kindly to being rousted in the middle of the night by a city driver."

Noora giggled. "We don't have bears here," she said, following Alek through the door. "They're out in the woods, silly, and hardly ever come to the village."

Alek turned around to her, then bent down. "But the city boy doesn't know that, and we don't want him to," she whispered.

Noora looked up, wide-eyed, at Michael, then giggled. "We have big bears, city boy." She spread her arms wide to show him how big. "Like that. With big teeth."

"In that case, maybe you should be the one to drive." He tossed Noora the keys, then scrambled off the porch, plowing through the snow until he got to the Jeep. By the time Alek made it over with Noora, Michael was sprawled out in the back, his feet casually across the seat and his arms folded casually over his chest. "You can drive, can't you, Noora?" he asked. "Oh, and try not to hit too many bumps, or go off the road into a ditch like Dr. Alek did today."

"No," Noora squealed. "I'm too young to drive. Except Papa does let me drive the snow machine sometimes." She threw the keys back to Michael. "So you have to drive."

"You expect me to drive through all those bears?" He shook his head. "That's not a good idea. I might actually drive right into one this big." He extended his arms to show Noora that his bear was bigger than hers. "I think I'd be safer back here, and let the bear get you." He tossed the keys back to her.

Noora scrambled right into the back of the Jeep, landing in Michael's lap. "And I'll let the bear get you, city boy." She giggled.

"But if the bear gets me and you're in the back

with me, doesn't that mean the bear will get you, too?" Noora and Michael both turned their heads at precisely the same time and looked at Alek, who was arranging her supplies on the passenger seat next to the driver's. "Looks like you're driving," he said as he took the keys from Noora and tossed them at Alek. "It's unanimous. You're driving and we're hiding. Just watch out for the bears."

The ride was short, and filled with laughs and giggles all the way. Alek was tempted to look back and see what all the fun was about, but the road was tricky—not so deep with snow, but there were drifts to avoid. And while her help in this childbirth was unsolicited, and most likely unneeded, she did want to get there in the event something went wrong.

So she didn't get to look back at Michael and Noora, but she could hear what was going on, and what she heard was amazing. Michael was a natural with Noora, and the child responded to him much the way everybody in the village had. More than that, Alek didn't get the impression that Michael was being anything other than genuine with Noora. He was doing magic tricks, pulling a coin out of her ear and hiding it in his hand, and laughing as hard as she was.

So maybe he wasn't quite so bad as she'd thought. A man that good with children couldn't be all bad. Still, there had been that day in class… A tirade like that aimed at a child could be devastating. She hadn't been close to being a child and it had been devastating to her.

Besides all that, there was his accusation about Dimitri. Everything else aside, that was what mattered most now. Being called inept was a small affair in contrast.

"It's a polar bear!" Michael suddenly shouted, then ducked down to the floor, pulling Noora down with him.

"We don't have polar bears here, city boy," Noora squealed, creeping back up and looking around to make sure there really weren't any sneaking up on them, even though she knew better. In the white of the snow, along with the bright of the moon, it was light outside, a perfect light, despite it being the middle of the night, and Noora glanced first to the right, then to the left before she finally gave Michael the signal that it was safe for him to come up, too.

"So what would it be if it's not a polar bear?" he asked, looking up at her from the floor.

"A snowshoe hare, silly." Noora giggled, then raised her hands to show how small it was.

"And you think I'd be afraid of a little thing like that?" He faked a scowl at her. "A little, tiny snowshoe hare? I think it was a polar bear."

"Or a tree." Noora giggled again. "A great big one that looks like a polar bear." She spread her arms to look like a tree, then growled like a bear at Michael, to which he responded by doing the same. And the two of them continued to growl at each other until Alek pulled to a stop outside Noora's house.

"So, besides your mother and grandmother, is anyone else here?" Alek asked, hopping out of the Jeep and grabbing her medical bag.

"No," Noora said. "It's Grandma and me. Oh, and my brother or sister, if my mama is better now."

"Someone needs to have a serious birds-and-bees talk with Noora," Michael commented, climbing out of the Jeep and attempting to straighten out his parka as Noora was tugging at him, trying to pull him back into the vehicle.

"Are you volunteering?" Alek asked, smiling

as he tried to extricate himself from the child. It was a cute sight.

"I treat trauma and illness quite nicely, but I think I'll leave the facts of life to her mother… or you."

Alek laughed. "Coward."

"For once, we agree."

"So how do you do it, Michael?" she asked, while Noora latched on to his leg as he maneuvered through the snow up to the front porch.

Before he answered, he bent down, picked up the little girl and tucked her neatly under his arm. "Do what?"

"That," Alek said, pointing to the laughing child. "One minute with her and she's yours for life."

"Good with children, good with animals. Most of the time good with adults."

Alek grabbed her bag of supplies and headed for the front door. "Not as good as you think!"

"I'm sensing a little hostility here, and just when I thought we were starting to get on."

Alek knocked on the front door, then turned to face him while she waited for someone to open it. "Not hostility. Merely a pointed observation. And we weren't getting on, Michael. Not when you're on the attack over Dimitri. We'll never get on because of that."

"You expect me to have an open mind, yet you don't? Isn't that a double standard, Doctor? You're entitled to your opinion but I'm not entitled to mine?"

"About Dimitri, no, you're not!"

"And the lady has two scores to settle with me now. One about which I know, and one she will not disclose. Well, here's my opinion, Alek, like it or not. I did you wrong somehow, and I shouldn't have. Dimitri is doing my mother wrong and I won't let him. I don't know all the facts about one incident, and you don't know all the facts about the other. My opinion is, we should go deliver a baby and forget the rest of it for now." Michael stepped around Alek and offered his hand to Mamie Igliak, Noora's grandmother, when she answered the door. Before Alek could even get in her greeting to the old woman, she was standing alone on the porch, watching the screen door slam shut right in front of her.

"No wonder your mother ran away to Alaska," she muttered, pushing back the door and stepping inside the tiny, wood-frame house. "If you were my son, I'd be running even further than Alaska."

By the time Alek reached the rear bedroom, Michael was already at Kitty Eyinck's bedside, taking her pulse, and Mamie was watching him adoringly, like a woman who was newly in love. Somehow, she wasn't surprised. Michael Morse had the charms to soothe…well, just about everybody. Everybody, that is, except her.

"Contractions?" she asked him. "How far apart are they?"

"Around a minute," Michael answered. "Mamie says they've been getting harder and faster for the past half hour. And that Kitty is right at nine months along."

"You've learned all that in ten seconds?" Alek questioned, opening up her bag and pulling out a pair of disposable gloves.

Michael laughed. "Actually, in the first five seconds. In the second five, Kitty told me she would like to have a boy, and that if she does they're going to name him something traditional, like Niyak, after Mamie's late husband, Niyak Igliak Eyinck."

Alek shook her head. Incredible, she thought.

Absolutely incredible. What were all these people seeing in him that she wasn't? "So how about I take a look? Or have you already done that, too?"

He grinned as he took hold of Kitty's hand during her latest contraction. "Did anybody ever tell you how cute you are when you're angry at me?"

"I really should have run over you when I had the chance," she muttered, pulling back the sheet from Kitty. A quick exam revealed that she was fully dilated, the baby was crowning and one brand-new Eyinck was anxious to get out into the world. "From the looks of things here, I'd say we're ready to go." She glanced over at Mamie, to make sure she wasn't offending the older woman. Around here, the use of a midwife in the delivery was much more common than calling the doctor to do the task, and the last thing she wanted to do was offend Mamie or Kitty over a delivery that appeared to be perfectly normal. Until their arrival, Mamie would have handled things quite well all by herself. "Mamie, would you like to do this, or shall I?"

Mamie was giggling over something Michael had said, or maybe he'd pulled a coin out of her ear like he had Noora's. Whatever the case, she gave Alek a dismissive wave of the hand and trotted off to the kitchen to fix Michael a cup of coffee, or perhaps make him a cake or a nice mooseburger, while Alek was left to… "Push, Kitty. With your next contraction, push."

That's exactly what happened. One push and the head was visible.

"Now stop pushing," Michael instructed. He was sitting casually on the side of the bed next to Kitty now, holding her hand and blotting the sweat from her face. Amazingly, he was keeping her calm. Without the benefit of an anesthetic agent, Kitty was absolutely serene through this whole ordeal. Another of Michael's amazing tricks. Alek wondered how many more he had. Bagsful, she bet.

"Now, your baby's head will rotate until Dr. Sokolov can make sure it's aligned with the shoulders, then she'll suction his mouth and nose to make sure he can get a good, deep first breath when he pops all the way out."

"Is it a boy, Doctor?" Kitty gasped, as she strained to sit up and take a look.

"Haven't seen that much yet, but I'm betting it is. A big one, too."

Alek shook her head impatiently as she palpated the baby's neck for the presence of a cord, which was not there. "I'll bet you're right at least half the time, aren't you?"

"At least," he said, grinning at her. He turned back to Kitty. "Now, start bearing down again. It's time we welcomed that baby to the world."

"Yes, Doctor," Kitty said, giving another hard push. Within a few seconds the shoulders, then the rest of the baby appeared, and seconds after that, after Alek had suctioned the nose and mouth, clamped and cut the cord, she laid the little boy on Kitty's belly. "It's a boy," she announced, as little Niyak wailed.

"Michael," Kitty said. "Michael Niyak Eyinck."

"Michael?" Alek sputtered. Kitty was looking alternately, and adoringly, from little Michael to big Michael as Mamie was toting in a cup of coffee for big Michael and showing him to an easy chair in the corner of the bedroom. An honored easy chair reserved only for Mr. Eyinck or, apparently, for Michael Morse now. "You named the baby Michael?"

CHAPTER SIX

"IT WAS Ben Smiling's stew," Alek explained to Dimitri while she stomped the snow off her boots. It was close to evening now, all the various medical problems were settled in Beaver Dam, and most likely Michael wasn't too far behind her. She'd convinced Aklanuk Mountain to delay the gasoline for an hour or two—not that the head start mattered, as Michael would eventually show up in Elkhorn. But getting the best of him did make her feel a little better. "Nothing serious, and no one too sick. Got them dosed, delivered Kitty Eyink's baby boy in the meantime, had a go at a pelvic exam for one of the village girls and got out of there." She stepped into Dimitri's open embrace, and hugged him. "And it's good to be home. Between the conference and staying over to order supplies, then going to Beaver Dam, it seems like I've been away for years."

"It's good to have you home, too," he said, chuckling. "And I always knew Ben's stew had the potential to poison a whole town. I've been telling him for years his no-good stew needed something other than beaver to make it fit for consumption. Nasty, stringy meat. Now, a nice buzhenina would be good."

"Except buzhenina isn't the tradition." Alek laughed. He'd spent his entire life here, yet Dimitri didn't exactly get along with the local fare. In that aspect, he was Russian all the way. "And Ben Smiling would never, ever put a fresh ham into his traditional stew, and you know that."

"Which is why I never go to Beaver Dam on Founder's Day. Because there's not a slice of buzhenina to be found anywhere."

"So tell me about her, Dimitri. The woman who answered your phone that one time when I called. She is the new doctor, isn't she? Except for hearing that she has a pleasant voice, that's all I know about her." *Except that she has a beast of a son.*

Alek felt his grip on her loosen a bit. Dimitri was definitely uncomfortable about this.

"She's nice," he conceded. "And, yes, she is the new doctor."

The man who was never of few words suddenly was, which spoke volumes to Alek. "She's nice, and…?"

"Pretty. Oh, and she's smart. She likes to read and listen to classical music. Tchaikovsky."

Getting information from Dimitri was harder than pulling Aryeh Tillion's tooth, if Aryeh Tillion had allowed her to do it. And there was so much caution in his voice. Normally, Dimitri boomed, but right now he was speaking in what would pass, in normal society, as a regular voice, maybe even one that was a bit subdued. The voice he'd always used with Olga. "So tell me more about her, Dimitri," she said, trying to sound chipper. "More than that she likes Tchaikovsky. Tell me how long you two have been…" Been what? She didn't know exactly. "And how you met, and what you have in common."

"We've been corresponding on the computer for about four months now. She was part of one of those chat rooms…one for older physicians. We dallied about in there for a while, talking about issues…aging, losing a spouse, how to continue our practice when medicine favors younger physicians. She was struggling trying to find herself again, and…"

"And you became friends?"

"We talked back and forth privately, yes. By e-mail at first. Out of the chat room after the first few weeks. Then we started phoning, and I had a brief little stay-over with her down in Vancouver last month when I went to look at a new X-ray machine."

Alek laughed. "I thought it was strange that you didn't send me, since you hate doing those kinds of things. *And* you didn't come back with any information for a new machine."

He grimaced, and his beard bobbled up and down. "She had lost her husband, I'd lost my wife. She needed a place to work, I needed someone to come here and work. She has a son, I have you…both of you are physicians, too. We have so many things in common, as it turned out. It seemed like there was more to bring us together than keep us apart."

"So she came here to see you, which is why you sent me away, isn't it? To have your time together and allow her to settle in without my interference."

"More than time together," he said quite seriously. "When she moved in, I wanted her to feel comfortable. Besides, you needed some time away from here. You work too much, and I do worry that you stay too isolated. So I would have asked you to go to the conference even if I hadn't invited Maggie up."

She laughed. "And so you threw me out the door, so to speak."

"For your own good."

"And yours, too, I think." She stood on tiptoe to give him a kiss on the cheek. "I'm happy for you, Dimitri. You've been getting a little stodgy lately, and having Maggie around is just what you need since I can already see that she makes you happy." She gave him a peck on the other cheek, then stepped back.

"Stodgy?" he roared, finally back to his normal volume, the one Alek liked most. "You're calling me stodgy? I could live another seventy years and even then not be as stodgy as you are now. If you want to see stodgy, I'd suggest a mirror." He grinned through his bushy white beard. "It's been good having her here, Alek. She works with me during the day, and in the evening—"

"Is this something I really want to hear?" Alek teased. She took his hand and they strolled into her cabin together.

"She's good to me, and not in the way you're thinking, although don't think a man my age can't appreciate that aspect of a relationship, because he certainly can, in the right time and place. But it's nice to have a friend my age around here again. And one of my background. I've missed that, and Maggie brings that to me now. I believe I offer her the same."

"Maggie?" As if she didn't know Maggie's last name—know it all too well. Still, she wanted to hear it.

"Dr. Maggie Morse, our new associate. She nursed her husband through cancer for two years and now that he's gone, she's ready to work again, but no one will hire her because of her age. She's sharp, bright and one of the finest physicians I've ever had the pleasure of working with, and she has perfect skills. Three years out of the field put her on the shelf, however, and I was the one bright enough to take her off it. And she fits right in. The regulars already love her. Loved her right off."

The way the villagers had loved Michael right off. The way Dimitri lit up when he talked about Maggie made Alek realize all the more that she simply couldn't let Michael Morse upset things here. "Well, I'm glad she's here." As much as she despised Maggie's son, she was already fond of Maggie, and she hadn't even met her. "And I'm glad you found her in the chat room," she said, giving Dimitri another hug. "You deserve some happiness."

"Are you sure you're okay with this, Alek? Because if you're not, you know I'd—"

She thrust out her hand to stop him. "I'm good, Dimitri. I promise, I'm really good," she said, giving his arm a reassuring squeeze.

"I'm the one who knows you best," he reminded her, "and what I'm seeing in your eyes is telling me something entirely different."

"You worry too much."

"Because I'm entitled to worry. And you know why I do."

Self-worth issues was what Dimitri called it. He was correct to a point, but over the years she'd gotten better. A little therapy to get to the root of her problem—she wasn't sure if it had helped, or merely enlightened her. Either way, it had had its effects, but not total control. "I'm fine," she said. "A little tired. Nothing to worry about."

"So, if you're really that fine, did you meet anyone at the conference who might have made you even better? Anyone male? A boyfriend? Perhaps a lover?"

Alek dropped down into her sofa and pulled her legs up under her. It wasn't much of a cabin, three modest rooms, but it was hers. All hers, and she loved every little speck of it. "I met a dozen salesmen who were more than happy to wine and dine me when they found out I was also on a shopping spree. And I met several physicians who practically ran away when they found out where I practiced. It seems that the northern territories and the single girl aren't exactly an enticing combination. Oh, and there was the concierge who must have felt terribly sorry for me being so pathetically alone all the time because he kept sending me little fruit baskets for one." She laughed. "So, no, I didn't find anyone but, then, I wasn't looking."

"And you should have been," Dimitri scolded. "If I recall, I put that at the top of your list—*have a good look around.*"

"I did, and I found some new acid reflux pill samples. And a new cholesterol-lowering drug that might be worth trying. And I think I've found a better intravenous delivery system than what we've been using. Oh, and—"

"Stodgy," Dimitri interrupted. "You send the girl to a medical conference, where everybody has some fun. And what does she do? She spends all her time with an IV system." He shook his head and ran his hand through his hair. "You are hopeless, Aleksandra. A woman contented to live in a tiny cabin alone, whose only companionship is her dog team, deserves a fruit basket for one." He bent and kissed her on the forehead. "Maggie is working right now, but she's anxious to meet you."

"When do you need me on shift?"

"Not until tomorrow morning. Mariska's on all night tonight and Maggie's taking the last shift while I take on-call, so we're fine."

Mariska, a local nurse trained by Dimitri, had been a fixture at the clinic for longer than Alek could remember. She and Eyanna, another nurse trained by Dimitri, ran the clinic, and they could not get along without them. They didn't have formal training—something Michael would undoubtedly call quackery if he found out. In spite of their lack of it, though, she would put their skills up against those of any other nurse anywhere because both of them were that good. Certainly, it was an unorthodox situation, but it worked.

There were several others who came to help from time to time—mostly volunteers looking for a way to pay for their medical services—and Michael would look at that as quackery, too, she supposed. But Dimitri never turned down a volunteer, and the volunteers were what kept this place up and running. So for such a remote area, they were well staffed, especially now that there were three physicians.

Of course, as the staff grew, so did the demand for their services, which was good because that meant more people in the area were seeking medical help. "Since everything is taken care of, and I'm assuming the reason you were here when I got home was to stock my refrigerator with whatever you want me to cook, I'll cook dinner for the two of you. Unless you have other plans." She gave him a little wink. "If you do, I'll certainly understand."

"Me turn down one of your dinners?" He snorted. "Not a chance. My only plans are to spend my evening with two beautiful women, eating a lot of food, like pelmeni, if that's what happens to be on the table when I get there." He walked to the door, then turned back to Alek. "I think Maggie's going to stay here with me permanently. It's not completely settled yet because she has some ideas she wants to work on, and I know I should have discussed this with you before I invited her, since this is your clinic, too. But I wasn't sure it would work out, and I didn't want to make too big a fool of myself. Especially since a man my age has no right to expect as much as I'm expecting."

"You have every right, Dimitri, and I'm glad your chat room worked out," she replied. "And I know I'll love her. But we need to talk about…" She couldn't do it. Not now. Michael would be here soon enough, and they'd sort it out when he was. Until then, she wanted Dimitri to stay as happy as he was right now.

Alek blew Dimitri a kiss. "We'll talk later. Now, get on back to that lady of yours before she finds another handsome Russian doctor to take your place."

* * *

"I've heard so much about you!" Maggie exclaimed an hour later as she hugged Alek. "And I'm glad to finally meet you after everything Dimitri has said."

Alek stepped back and couldn't help but stare. Maggie Morse was the exact image of her son—same charming smile, same twinkling green eyes, same slightly curly brown hair, close cut without a single strand of gray. Beautiful woman, striking, vibrant…no wonder Dimitri had been taken with her so quickly. She had what Michael had. "Well, he didn't tell me nearly enough about you," she responded, giving Dimitri an approving wink. "Not nearly enough."

"Something we'll soon fix," Maggie said, latching on to Dimitri's arm as they crossed into the great room of Alek's cabin. "Because I'm hoping that we'll become good friends." She glanced up adoringly at Dimitri. "Since we both share an affection for the same man."

True love unfolding right before her eyes. Alek had never seen it before. She didn't recall anything of her mother, and she'd never seen her father involved romantically. She'd seen love between Dimitri and Olga, but it had been a long-standing kind, one of people who had always loved each other and grown mellow in it. What she saw now was young and fresh, and in a way she envied them.

And she worried, because Michael was going to ruin it if he could. "I'm sure we'll be great friends," she said in all sincerity, even though she wasn't sure how long it would last once Michael arrived. "So how about we feed this man we both adore, and get to know each other better over pelmeni, draniki, svejie ovoshy and—?"

"And it can only be pumpkin oladi," Dimitri exclaimed, practically licking his lips. "She gives me my favorite meal, and now I can only wonder why."

Alek latched on to the arm Maggie didn't have hold of and gave him a squeeze. "Partly because you stocked it in my refrigerator, but mostly because I missed you."

"Then you should go away and come back more often," he teased, leading both his ladies into the kitchen.

"And here I am, barely able to boil water," Maggie said, taking her seat. "My poor Michael…" She glanced up at Alek. "My son," she explained, then continued, "He didn't have the benefit of many home-cooked meals, I'm afraid. I couldn't cook, and didn't particularly like it even if I could. And my husband was even worse than I was. So Michael learned to cook, which was a saving grace for us because if it hadn't been for him we would have eaten nothing but sandwiches. But Michael could have gone to culinary arts school, he was so good."

"And my Aleksandra is magnificent in the kitchen," Dimitri said, beaming. "Almost as good a chef as she is a doctor. Just like your Michael."

"Which is a good thing," Maggie added, then laughed, "because at my age, I don't particularly care to learn fine arts in the kitchen. Sandwiches, takeout food, a can of soup…those were always fine for me after my husband was gone and Michael moved out, especially the takeout, although I'm betting I won't find much of that around here."

"But I always have a can of soup to share," Dimitri said, then gave Alek a wink. "When I can't convince my Aleksandra to cook for me."

"His way of convincing me is to show up at mealtimes," Alek said. "It's a good thing I love to cook for an army because Dimitri loves to eat like one. And you're always welcome," she said to Maggie. "Even when I'm not here, there's usually something in the refrigerator. The cabin door's never locked, so feel free to help yourself."

"You've raised a nice young lady," Maggie said.

"I've raised a magnificent young lady," Dimitri responded. "And, lucky for me, a magnificent cook."

Dimitri and Maggie chatted on while Alek served up the mincemeat-sausage dish, along with the potato pancakes and the cucumber, tomato and onion salad, and by the time she finally took her seat the conversation was long past Maggie's lack of domestic skills and well into one of Dimitri's tales of an adventure somewhere north of the Arctic Circle—exactly how far depended on Dimitri's mood when he was telling it. "We were floating on a one-man raft, just the three of us on the Jim River."

Alek smiled as the story progressed. It was one of her favorites, and now Dimitri had a brand-new audience for the tales of his escapades. She was happy for him.

"Didn't see a bear anywhere. Not a single one. But there was this big old cow moose, and she took a liking to me. Followed us along on the shore for a good while with love in her eyes, and there's nothing more frightening than a cow moose with love in her eyes. Especially when you know that look is for you. I'd rather have tangled with a bear than that little lady."

Dinner was pleasant, and somewhere into the *svejie ovoshy* Alek learned that Maggie was not only a doctor, she was a surgeon. And Michael had been perpetuating a myth of helplessness about her. Apparently, he hadn't paid much attention to his mother because she was anything but the helpless, vulnerable woman he'd described.

"You may have taken your wilderness certification classes from him, Alek," Maggie said, snapping Alek back into the conversation.

"I'm sorry?"

"My son, Michael. He teaches wilderness classes in Seattle, and Dimitri said you went down there a few years ago to get your certification. So maybe you ran into him, or even took one of his classes. His name is—"

Before Maggie could utter his name, there was a sharp knock at the door and Alek had the sinking feeling that he, whom she would prefer would remain nameless, was the one knocking. She glanced at her watch. He'd made amazing time. She really hadn't expected him until after the pumpkin oladi.

"Want me to get it?" Dimitri asked, starting to stand.

"Good heavens, no!" Alek exclaimed, practically falling out of her chair to beat him to it. "You stay there and enjoy your supper. I'll take care of whoever's out there."

"I'm on call this evening," Dimitri said, as he speared another plump pelmeni. "We've got two nurses on, but if someone needs a doctor…"

Before he finished, Alek ducked out of the room and into the entry hall, wishing now she had a much larger cabin, one where she could actually hide Dimitri and Maggie while Michael came in ranting and raving. Which was exactly what he was about to do.

Slowly, she opened the door a crack, and took a peek outside.

"Alek," he said, surprisingly civil, all things considered.

"Michael," she choked, inching her eyes from

his toes upward, ever so slowly, since she really didn't want to see the frown there.

"Aren't you going to invite me inside? It's been a long, cold trip from Beaver Dam, and I believe you owe me a little hospitality after the delay you put me through."

Her eyes stopped at his kneecaps. "No," she said, tying to sound forceful about it. "I can't invite you in. Not tonight. Maybe tomorrow." Then she tried shutting the door, but he pushed it back at her.

"I intend sleeping here," he stated, still maintaining his place outside on the porch. "In your cabin, since Elkhorn doesn't have a hotel, in case you didn't know that. But I stopped at the hospital, told them I was a doctor, and they pointed me in your direction."

Her eyes inched on up his legs and stopped near his chest. "I don't have a guest room, Michael, but the hospital has rooms. I'll call over there and make arrangements—"

"I want these arrangements, Alek. Your cabin. You owe me that much."

His voice was so deep, so quiet, so sexy, it caused her to shiver.

"And I'm not even going to bring up the fact that you persuaded the good people of Beaver Dam to delay me so you could get here first. Nice try, but I haven't changed my mind."

Finally, her eyes reached his, and they were narrowed, yet still twinkling. How could that be? Angry yet…yet what? She hadn't seen that look before, and once again she shivered, and not from the cold. "Your mother is where she wants to be."

"She's inside, isn't she?"

She wouldn't lie. "Having supper."

"And I'm not invited?"

He arched one eyebrow at her, and if she hadn't known better, she would have almost thought this a prelude to seduction. But this was Michael, which meant that it was, more likely, a prelude to an outburst. With that in mind, she took a firmer grip on her door. "No," she stated flatly. "You're not invited. The woman is an intelligent, sensible physician and you go on about her like she's a feeble, dithering old woman."

"So you're attempting to hide her from me." He chuckled, but it was so low she could barely hear it. Although she could feel it all the way down to her toes. "Like I said before, Alek, nice try, but I haven't changed my mind."

"I'm going to let her eat a meal in peace before you ruin her digestion. Afterward, if she wants to see you, I'll let her know you're staying at the hospital. Under lock and key in our psychiatric ward." Of course, they didn't have a psychiatric ward, but the little threat did sound good.

"You threaten the lock and key an awful lot," he taunted. "As an officer of the law, as a physician."

"Get off my porch," Alek snarled. "Get off right now, or I'll show you what this officer of the law can do with her lock and key."

He actually grinned at her—a big, bodacious grin that said he didn't take a thing about her seriously. "And that, Alek, is one more reason to get my mother out of all this lunacy, which is what it is when someone like you has the power to arrest someone like me. So let's just make this easy on both of us. Let me in."

"Fine. Do what you want. But let me warn you, Michael, your mother is happy here, and she won't be going home with you." She hoped. For Dimitri's sake, she surely did hope.

"Michael! I thought I heard your voice,"

Maggie said as she stepped around the corner into the hallway.

"He came to kidnap you," Alek muttered.

Maggie laughed aloud. "He's always been so protective of me. Especially since his father died." She stepped around Alek, and went to kiss her son. "I appreciate your concern, Alek, but I promise, Michael's not going to take me anywhere."

As the two stood in the doorway, exchanging greetings, Alek returned to the table. "It's Michael Morse," she said glumly. "And I really wanted to talk to you about this a little while ago, but you were so happy, and I just couldn't."

"So talk to me now," Dimitri said, lowering his voice so it was barely above a whisper.

"He was with me in Beaver Dam. I met him at the four-way and he followed me there. And he's not a nice man, Dimitri. He's determined to take his mother home because he thinks you're…" It was so difficult to say the next words. She couldn't, because she would not hurt Dimitri. Not for anything. "Because he thinks she's not ready for an involvement."

"So Michael's protecting Maggie and you're protecting me? Is that what's going on here?"

"Something like that, only I wasn't very good at it. Look, he's a mean-spirited man. I know he's Maggie's son, and that you and Maggie are, well, whatever it is that you are, and he's an excellent doctor, but he's going to cause trouble, Dimitri."

"Which you don't think I can handle?"

"Which I don't think you should have to handle. Maybe you should go out the back door right now, put off meeting him for a while, because I think he's probably in a horrible mood."

"Something you did to him?"

Alek laughed halfheartedly. "I suppose you could say that."

Dimitri dropped his napkin onto the table, then stood. "I'm not running away from Maggie's son, Alek. What I am going to do, though, is go take over her last round at the clinic so she can spend the rest of the evening with Michael. Tell her she can bring him over to meet me when she's ready. Oh, and find a place for the man to stay, will you? Maggie's in my second bedroom or I'd ask him to stay there. Take care of him. Get him settled in. Get him settled down." He gave her a cheery wink. "Give him a pelmeni."

"Why?"

"To show him there's more to you than your pretty face." Dimitri ducked through the kitchen and out the back door while Alek sat at the table, looking at the leftover pelmeni on the platter. It would take more than a sausage to settle Michael Morse—settle him in *or* settle him down.

"Where's Dimitri?" Maggie asked as she came back to the table, followed by Michael.

"He took your last round for the night," she replied, looking up at Michael for any sign of hostility. But she couldn't read his face. He was smiling, his eyes seemed pleasant, but...but she didn't know. "Care for a pelmeni, Michael?" she asked, for a lack of anything better to say.

"He shouldn't be taking my shift since he's on call later," Maggie said. "Besides, he's had a long few days, so I think I'll go on over and help him finish. Look, Michael, take Maggie up on her dinner offer. It's wonderful. She cooks as well as you do. So eat, enjoy, and we'll talk later." She let go of his arm and headed to the door. "Oh, and you'll need to find a place to stay the night, Michael. Maybe Alek can make a suggestion." With that, Maggie hurried after Dimitri, leaving the two of them alone.

"So, are you going to arrest me?" he asked.

"I haven't decided." He stood in the doorway, filling up most of the space of it. She hadn't realized how large he was until now, until he became such an imposing figure in her cabin. "You can't do this, Michael. You can't force your mother to leave."

"But I can persuade. And I will, Alek."

"She cares for Dimitri."

"Because he gives her something she thought she'd lost. But once she sees that she doesn't need to find it here in Alaska, she'll leave."

"Or not. She has her work, and she and Dimitri have a good relationship going. So why *persuade* her to leave? Why interfere with what could be real happiness for her?" Alek pushed herself away from the table. "Have some pelmeni," she said, pointing to the platter. "And draniki and svejie ovoshy. Have all of it. Stuff yourself till you choke on it!"

"And what are you going to do? Go hide my mother from me again?"

"I'm going to the hospital to take over her shift so Dimitri and Maggie can have their time together, since you seem bent on taking that away from them." With that, she left the room and left Michael standing there looking over a dinner that certainly hadn't gone the way she'd planned.

"No, I insist," Alek said. "I need to get back to work, and now's as good a time as any."

"And Michael?" Dimitri asked, taking off his white lab coat and hanging it over the peg by the door in his cramped little office. Everything about the clinic was cramped—patient space was limited, the lab space was actually a converted storage room and the surgery wasn't much larger than the laboratory. It was a compact little facility, but tidy. Lately, though, it had been undersized for the growing needs of the area.

"I left him choking on dinner. I hope!"

"I understand your animosity, Alek. But something tells me it runs far deeper than you trying to protect me from him. Normally you're not so moody, but that's what you've been since you returned home. Moody. Downright grumpy. And that's not like you."

"Where Michael Morse is concerned, it is like me. I don't like him, Dimitri. I didn't when he was my instructor in Seattle, and I don't now.

But I'm not going to make an issue over it because I don't want to hurt Maggie. She doesn't deserve that." She tugged on her own lab coat and checked the pocket for her stethoscope. Finding it, she pulled it out and looped it around her neck. "I really do like her and I promise I'll do my best not to let her know that I absolutely despise her son."

"You're protesting awfully hard, aren't you? I seem to recall an old saying about the lady protesting too much."

"Trust me, he's worth the protest."

"Well, I don't know about that, but he certainly has captured the protester's attention, hasn't he?"

"He's like a light switch, Dimitri. Off and on. Problem is, you don't know when he's going to make a switch. And I know this puts you in a spot, because Maggie is probably telling you one thing about him while I'm telling you another, but she's his mother. She has to say nice things."

"And you don't. So why the fuss, Alek? Because all this bother about someone who will be gone in a few days seems rather reactionary to me." He grinned. "Olga hated me at first. Did I ever tell you that? She thought I was blustery and pompous, which I was. And she fought me… Dear God, how that woman fought me."

"So how did you two end up together?"

"Our parents were from the old country. It was an arranged marriage, and our parents forced us to go through with it."

That was a surprise, because while Alek couldn't remember Dimitri and Olga as a particularly happy couple, she'd always seen true devotion between them. Which, for them, could have been their happiness, she supposed. "How long did it take you two to, well…work it out?"

"I'd like to say our wedding night, but the truth is she locked me out of the bedroom." He chuckled. "And she was smart enough to nail shut the windows. Next morning, though, she did her wifely duty…"

Alek held up her hand to stop him.

"Breakfast," he said hastily. "Her wifely duty was breakfast, and I complimented her, even though it was an abominable failure—burnt toast, runny eggs . I think that was the first time I'd ever seen her smile. Then I complimented her on supper, and breakfast the next morning. And for the way she tidied the house and fixed her hair. It took a while, but we finally became friends—talked in the evening instead of glaring across the room at each other, went for walks. Eventually it turned into love."

"And the moral of the story is?" she asked, even though she knew. Dimitri was up to his matchmaking again. In spite of her feelings about Michael Morse, he was pairing the two of them.

"No moral. I thought you should know that love happens in different ways. Since you've never put yourself out there to try it—"

"You're wrong," she interrupted. "This isn't one of your different ways of love."

"Well, let me say that the last time I saw you in such a flap was when you came home from his wilderness classes. You were just like you are now…ready to wrestle a Kodiak bear with your bare hands, and pity the poor Kodiak."

"He rubs me the wrong way."

"Maybe the problem is, you've never given him a chance to rub you the right way. But I suppose you'll tell me what this is about when you're ready, won't you?"

"There's nothing to tell."

"You're not a good liar, Alek." He stepped

closer, then pulled her into his arms. "Always so brave and defiant, aren't you? Through all the heartache you've had, you've always tilted your head up and faced whatever there was. No tears, no complaints and always daring the world to try and come at you again. Someday, though, you've got to stop fighting. Someday you've got to allow yourself to let someone in—someone besides me. And also give yourself permission to let yourself out."

CHAPTER SEVEN

THE clinic was so quiet and yet so alive. Alek always marveled at the changes from day to night when she stepped through the doors. She loved it this way because it felt intimate and safe. The traumas of the day, whatever they might have been for her patients, were over and now it was time to settle in.

Hospitals big and small had their own distinct rhythms—some charged ahead full steam twenty-four hours a day. Others, especially in the harsher urban settings, sprang to life at night when the trauma departments became the hub of unfortunate activity. And Dimitri's little hospital woke up in the morning to a steady, laid-back pace—not fast, not frantic, not un-yielding—and continued that way throughout the day with minor surgeries, tests and other di-agnostic procedures, an array of therapies, routine patients needing shots and other supportive care.

Then in the evening, the hospital settled down to rest. Visitors wandered in for a friendly chat, routine tests were put away, shades were drawn, lights were dimmed. Maybe this was why she loved this time of the day in the tiny hospital best of all, and why she took night duty much more than her share. It fit her own natural rhythm. She chuckled. Of course, there were those weeks of the midnight sun when the light of day was endless, as well as those months of endless night when the tiny specks of daylight were a welcome relief. That was a rhythm unto itself, and one she loved as well. But now, at the time of year when the days and nights were more equal, she enjoyed the change from one to the other but found her greatest comfort in the quieter hours.

Tonight was a normal night and there were only ten patients in the wards, none of them very ill. One was on watch for an ulcer, another for a migraine headache. Two were in for general gastric upsets, and there were three children in the children's ward who were being looked over for respiratory difficulties. The rest of the patients were merely general aches and complaints, and Dimitri gave them beds more as a placebo than from any medical requirement, because they needed to know that somebody cared.

In the Romonov Clinic nobody was ever turned away, not even for a simple hangnail. It was the old country doctor way—the way Dimitri had always practiced. Take care of more than the complaint—take care of the whole patient. And sometimes that care turned out to be nothing more than a warm bed for the night and an attentive ear when one was needed.

Alek was spoiled by this kind of medicine now, and listening to the many lectures at the conference from which she'd just returned reminded her that medicine wasn't done this way in too many places these days. It was rushed and overcrowded and often impersonal. But here it was still a kinder, gentler way, and it was the only way she knew how to practice. Or wanted to practice. For all her years in medical school, Dimitri was the best teacher because he taught her true compassion and humanity—medical attributes that could not be gleaned from a textbook.

"Anyone need anything?" Alek asked Mariska,

who was scurrying her way down to the children's ward to tuck them in with sugar cookies and a bedtime story.

"Fine for the night, Alek," Mariska replied. "I've got two patients still up and playing chess in the waiting room and another one watching television. Everybody else is in bed, reading or sleeping, except the kiddies, who are fussing for their story." She handed Alek a cookie. "And these."

Alek took a bite of the cookie, and smiled. "Can you blame them? I'd be fussing for one of these, too."

Mariska, with her stark black hair pulled back tightly into a knot, was a large-boned woman who lumbered her way through the clinic with the authority of a military general. But she was a real softie with her nighttime cookies and stories and usually it wasn't only the children who partook. "You haven't changed, Alek. Not since you were a little girl, always coming around to beg my cookies."

"And you always gave me one or two, didn't you?"

Mariska chuckled. "You wouldn't have gone

away until I did because you were as stubborn then as you are now."

"Well, I'm going to take my stubborn self down to the wards and have a look, then go to Dimitri's office to catch up on that stack of charts he doesn't like to mess with." Anything to avoid going back to her cabin, back to Michael, in case he was still there.

"Hiding from that man in your house?"

"What makes you think there's a man in my house?" Other than the fact that news spread fast in Elkhorn.

"There's got to be something keeping you from going home when you take to figuring out Dimitri's charts. I was guessing it was that man you dragged back here from Beaver Dam. The good-looking one who came around looking for you a little while ago."

"I didn't drag. He followed," she protested, trying to sound more indifferent than affected.

"But good-looking is good-looking. And you're missing out on all that for some lousy paperwork." She clucked her tongue. "Those charts won't keep you warm on a long, cold Alaska night, Alek."

"But I have a nice woolen blanket that will."

"Stubborn, like I said. And the older you get, the more stubborn you're becoming. We're all worried about you, Alek. Sometimes you look so unhappy."

"I'm not," she whispered. Not really. But sometimes she did wish for…she wasn't sure what. "One more cookie?" she asked, forcing a smile.

Two hours later, sitting at Dimitri's desk with half the waiting folders now in the "work completed" pile and the single light from the desk lamp the only thing keeping her from falling asleep over the remaining charts, Alek finally shut off the light, then almost crawled over to the small sofa in the corner of the office and curled up on it. Sure, she could go home and be more comfortable, but why bother? If he was still there, she'd have to see Michael, have to talk to him, have to deal with him in some fashion, and she simply didn't want to. So maybe avoiding him was only a temporary solution, because at some point she'd have to face the inevitable. However, right now she was too tired to come up with a better idea.

Alone. He'd come here to find his mother. That's all he'd ever intended. Find her, take her home, put this whole Alaskan experience behind them. And now here he was, alone in Alek Sokolov's cabin, washing dishes for a dinner he hadn't eaten, while his mother was off with Dimitri, doing who knew what. And so far he hadn't even met Dimitri. That was the kicker. His mother was protecting the man as much as Alek was. "And here I am, standing at the sink scraping dried potato pancake off a stack of plates. So it's not going according to plan," he muttered, as he submerged a large cast-iron skillet into the sudsy warm water.

The other thing that hadn't gone according to plan had been the look on his mother's face. She looked happy. Positively radiant. He hadn't seen that spark in her eyes since before his father had gotten sick, hadn't seen her smile so much since then, either. What had he expected to find? Well, he hadn't thought that far ahead. Maybe a dull look, or one of confusion, or the unmistakable look of someone being duped. But now he was in the indecision of a rethink over his pots and pans. Maybe he'd get to know Dimitri before he tried convincing his mother to leave because maybe, just maybe, Alek was right about him. "Which would make me wrong."

Yes, that was it. Have a chat with the man and try to see through his intentions. That would be fair to his mother, if nothing else. Stay here another day and actually see what it was about Dimitri Romonov that was making her happy.

And face Alek. He did owe her that much, he supposed.

Michael glanced up at the woodblock clock on the wall as it was audibly clicking its way from minute to minute. He was a late-nighter, and it was still early. Too early to settle in, even if he did have a place in which to settle down. "So what do they do for fun in Elkhorn?" he mused, as he tossed the apron he'd been wearing over onto the counter and rolled down his shirt-sleeves. There was no one on the street, he noticed as he glanced out the kitchen window. No one there at all. Not even a stray dog, looking for a full garbage can. And naturally it was snowing again. Not hard, but quite steadily, probably adding another few inches to what was already there.

"Any ideas?" he asked one of Alek's team

dogs lurking outside the window. Earlier, he'd tossed the pelmeni out to the pack, and now they were huddling about, waiting for the oladi, which he had finished himself. "Other than going to bed and figuring it out tomorrow?" He smiled over the thought of taking Alek's bed. She would rile up quite nicely once she found him in it. "Then make me sleep in the kennel with you," he said through the window to the pack as he turned out the kitchen light and strolled into the front room.

Alek's bed…her sheets. Yes, he could almost see himself stretched out between them. They would be practical white, of course. Nothing about Alek was impractical. But pink would suit her…he could almost see her black hair against a pink pillowcase. Beautiful contrast.

She would never indulge in pink, though. Pity, because it would suit her. And now that he'd thought about it, he wanted to have a look—only to see if he was right about her white sheets. Feeling like a thief sneaking in to steal a prized possession, Michael quietly entered her bedroom, pulled back the comforter atop her bed and took a look. Sure enough, white. Just like he'd thought. Plain white. And…was that lavender? Did he really smell lavender?

"Well, well, Alek. You do indulge yourself a little, don't you?" Plain, practical Aleksandra Sokolov washed her sheets in lavender water. "Not quite as tough as nails as you let on, are you?" He smiled as he returned to the living room, thinking about what it would be like to stretch out between those sheets that mingled with the crisp scent of lavender and Alek.

Simply to annoy her, he probably should. Except that he wanted to…a little too much. Which was a problem, because he shouldn't want to. And the little tug that made him want to crawl right in, and even fantasize about doing it, was a concern.

"Time to get the hell out," he muttered. "Need some good, cold air." It had the same effect as a good, cold shower when he stepped outside. A nice, brisk walk up the street, then back down did the trick, but ten minutes later he found himself standing on the front walk of the Romonov Clinic, debating over whether he should go in or continue to impress the first footprints on the new snow from one end of town to the other. Alek wouldn't want him there, which made the idea of intruding on her seem appealing. She did taunt so well, didn't she? It was almost arousing, the way she always came right back at him. Another time in his life this could have been so different. Sadly, at this time it was only what it was.

A shadow in the window at the corner of the wood-frame building caught his attention. Someone was in there, someone who was moving slowly about the office. The form was vague, the gender impossible to discern, but he stayed fixed on the movements until the light inside was turned off. He knew it was Alek. He couldn't see her. But he knew. Or felt it. Sensed it, maybe. Even though he didn't understand why, since every strand of common sense inside him was warning him away, he went inside the clinic, straight down the hall to that corner office.

The dimmed hallway was deserted, not a person in sight. But all along the empty corridor he could hear far-off sounds…children giggling, deeper voices chatting quietly, perhaps the television droning away. By the time he reached the short stretch leading to the office where he knew he would find her, the noises had dissipated into a soft buzz, and the only real discernible sound was that of his own footsteps clicking on the tile floor. It was an eerie, hollow sound, his steady repetitive pounding, and by the time he approached the office, he'd actually measured the rhythm of his steps, trying hard to mark off those last meters to her door in a precise, rhythmic cadence instead of concentrating on what he had to do…to say.

But it was time. It wasn't easy, but he owed it to her, and she deserved it.

Raising his hand to knock, Michael gave it another thought and instead merely walked in, then took a moment, standing in the doorway, to allow his eyes to adjust to the total darkness.

She was in here. He couldn't see her yet. But that strange sense of presence was returning, the one that made him acutely aware of Alek, the one that raised the hair on the back of his neck just the slightest. *So, what the hell is this?* he asked himself as he leaned against the door frame and folded his arms across his chest. Why was merely being in the same room with her so disquieting?

Alek watched him stand in the doorway, backlit by the dim light of the hall coming in over his shoulder. He wasn't moving, wasn't coming in or going out. He wasn't encroaching in any way, other than standing there. Which, in a sense, did encroach because as long as he was there, she was forced to be alert, to watch him as he did her, wondering what would come next. Who would make the first move? Would he speak? Should she? Would he take another step through the door, or should she stand to greet him?

This was a ridiculous mix of emotions—uncertainty, anger, and something she refused to label in any way because, in spite of everything, she was still attracted to him, like she had been the first time she'd seen him. That long, lonely drive from Beaver Dam with Michael on her mind every kilometer of the way hadn't helped, because by the time she'd pulled into her driveway she'd reached the conclusion that it was, unfortunately, some leftover, unresolved attraction brought on by the fact that she hadn't even thought about another man the way she'd thought about him all those years ago. It was a shock, realizing that she could feel that strongly for him in so many different ways, but she wasn't going to be silly about this thing and merely brush it off to being overwrought, too tired, or just plain loopy. *She was attracted.* Of course, it was only a chemical reaction, and she'd been quick to tack that on to her wobbly reasoning. His hormones versus hers. She was a doctor, and she certainly understood pure sexual physiology at its best. Or its peskiest.

Problem was, it was taking hold in a much larger way than it should have. Her heart rate was faster than usual, and her breathing a little unsteady. Although that could be anger—another addendum to her recent reasoning on the subject of Michael Morse. And she was angry after all. In spite of all the other confused feelings twirling around inside, she was *very* angry at him.

"I finally remembered you," he said, his voice so quiet and smooth it nearly blended into the dark of the room. "And the funny thing was, when I did, I realized that I'd never forgotten you. Merely put you away as part of a dreadful time in my life. Sometimes it's easier to not remember, you know. Past deeds, past offenses, people who didn't deserve what you did to them, just put it all away and go on from there."

"And how am I supposed to react to that,

Michael? Be gracious? Tell you it doesn't matter anymore? Say that it wasn't a big deal at the time? Because I'm not gracious. It still does bother me and it was a big deal at the time." Especially since more than her professional pride had been hurt by him.

"You're supposed to react any way you want, Alek. That day in class…" He drew in a deep, shuddering breath. "I'm sorry for that. And the truth is, I really *don't* remember it."

"Funny how that selective amnesia works well for you, isn't it? Remember me, don't remember me. Remember what you did to me that day, don't remember."

He laughed bitterly. "You're close, but it wasn't amnesia. It was drugs."

Alek gasped. "What?" she choked.

"Drugs. Amphetamines. And there's no excuse for what I did. I got caught up, simple as that. There weren't enough hours in the day to accomplish everything I needed to do, then not enough hours to sleep after I had done it all. Something had to give, and it was my reasoning, my common sense. I knew what I was doing, too, Alek. Take a pill in the morning to get me going, take another at night to let me sleep. It's amazing how easy it becomes. There's instant energy when you need it, and instant sleep when you don't. And you tell yourself you're going to take this one pill and that's all. No more. But it's never only one, there's always more. Tomorrow you need another, and then the next day another. And why not make that two since one seems to work so well? Get yourself more energy, get yourself better sleep.

"Then pretty soon you need an extra one…something in the middle of the day to tide you over. And you justify it by looking at all the extra work you're getting done. More hours at the hospital, an expanded teaching schedule, more interviews, another book. And the hell of it was, I recommended patients into detox for taking less than I was. Of course, I didn't have a problem. I could quit anytime I wanted. Right?"

"Michael, I'm so sorry. That day in class…"

"I'm so sorry for that, Alek. Drugs, stress… I'd learned that my dad had been diagnosed with cancer, and I snapped. Which is no excuse for what I did to you. And I wouldn't have treated you that way if I hadn't been full of drugs. But that wasn't me. That was the horrible creature the drugs created, the one who couldn't see that what he did and what he said was so often out of control."

"Are you okay now?"

"Yes," he said quietly. "And it wasn't easy, because the one illusion I always had of myself was that I was strong. Stronger than just about anybody. But when you crave that pill more than the oxygen you breathe, you come to understand how weak you really are. And I wasn't a saint. Even after that day, I didn't want a cure. I wanted to deny it, pretend it was just a way to see me through the stress, then when it was over I'd be okay. Excuses. When you're addicted, excuses are so easy. But the truth is, I've been off them only a year now. Which isn't very noble, since I should have done it long before that."

"When you quit, was it for yourself? It wasn't forced on you or anything like that, was it?"

"It was for myself. It has to be in order to work. I was addicted, Alek, and I didn't want to be, but I was the one who got me into that condition, and I was the one who had to get me out of it." It was so easy, talking to her. He'd never talked to anyone about this before, not a friend, not his parents. He'd simply checked himself into a clinic one day and done what had to be done. "I was hitting some real low spots long before I got help. One of which you became victim to. And the only reason I even knew what I'd done was because I was taping all my classes in order to come up with some good footage to develop a long-distance continuing education program. I didn't go back and review the tapes for quite a while and when I did… Let's just say that I lost sleep over it."

"So did I," she said quietly. "And I doubted my abilities, and agonized over how what you said could have ruined my reputation."

"God, I'm sorry, Alek. No wonder you've hated me. Believe me, I would have apologized. I've gone back to so many people and done that. Except I didn't know who they all were. There were so many classes, so many students, and that tape was a jumble, no identifiers to tell me when or who. I really intended to do the research and find you, but my dad took a turn for the worse, and I decided it was time to go straight. My life was one sorry mess, and I simply forgot." He laughed bitterly. "It's an easy thing to do in the condition I was in, and I'm surprised you came back and sat through another class with me."

"To be honest, so am I. But I wanted the certificate, and I decided not to let you bully me out of it. After that, though, you never said a word to me, never called on me again, never even looked at me in passing in the hall. Which was for the best. So how is it that you're remembering me now?"

"I knew whatever I'd done to you had to be horrible, so I started going over all the horrible things I've done, and I kept coming back to what I'd seen on that tape. I didn't want that to be you, didn't want it to be anybody I would ever have to face. But it was you, and I guess deep down I knew that. Then the more I thought about your reaction to me and the things you were saying, the more I knew. You were the one who sat in the back row, in the near-dark, and challenged me. The one who always questioned my ways, questioned my teaching, questioned the techniques I was trying to get across to the class. And you were the brightest one to ever come to one of my classes."

"It's true that I didn't always agree with you. But I wouldn't have said I was challenging you so much as asking for clarification."

He chuckled. "Clarification is a broad interpretation of the word."

"So maybe I challenged a little."

"A lot."

"Moderately."

"Moderately," he agreed. "You were in the same place for every single lecture, always apart from the rest of the class."

Sitting up, she watched him stand in the doorway, still making no attempt to enter. "Because I *was* apart from the class, Michael. Their idea of wilderness medicine was doing a little patch-up job during a day trip into the woods while I was hitching up my dog team and mushing out to a village to treat a small outbreak of TB. Different worlds, and we had nothing in common. It was easier that way."

"Back then you had short hair, like mine, didn't you? And huge glasses…"

"Corrective eye surgery. Glasses in the wild are an inconvenience."

"And you were a little heavier."

"Lots of hard work since then. Not much time to eat all the things I cook for Dimitri."

"You also smiled. Which you don't now. And

you were nice on the couple of occasions we chatted in the hall. A little defiant in some of your questions, but nice."

"Which I'm not now," she supplied.

"You have a harder edge now, yes. And maybe that's what threw me the most, because in spite of the way you came after me in class, *and you did,* you were always nice about it."

"Then you took the dagger to my throat."

"Because you stood out. The only one who did. You knew as much if not more than me, and in my hazy mind I think I was threatened by you. My life was coming apart, the amphetamine habit was out of control, and there you were, sitting in the back row, so sure of yourself when I was anything but sure. That's what I wanted to be, Alek. You! And I wasn't, so you got the brunt of my anger and frustration that day because it was the worst day of my life and I wanted someone else to hurt the way I did. I'm so sorry, and I have no reason to think that you'll accept my apology. But I hope you will."

"I do forgive you that incident, Michael. I've seen it happen to so many doctors—saw it in med school, saw it throughout my residency. The pressures are hard and I'd be lying if I said I didn't consider popping a pill a time or two back then. A lot of doctors, and would-be doctors, do it. I happened to be one who didn't. So I understand what you were going through, and I admire the fact that you got yourself through it. I only wish I'd known at the time. It wouldn't have been so…difficult."

"I wish I'd known at the time, too. And don't admire me. I'm still going through it. Only differently now that I don't take the pills."

"Are you ever tempted to relapse?"

"Sure, I've been tempted. That demon begging for just one pill is always there. I don't think it ever goes away."

"And maybe it shouldn't. Our experiences mold us into who we are. You're a good doctor. I saw that in the village. And it's not only your doctoring skills that are good. It's the other things—the way you make people comfortable, the way you listen. The way you…" Disarm them. Damn, she was playing right into his hands. Tell her his story, she'll take pity and back off. Well, not a chance. "You know what, Michael? You were in a bad place and did an admirable thing, and I'm over that part of not liking you. I do sincerely accept your apology. But, trust me, you've replaced that motive for not liking you with another one, and it's even stronger." She pulled a throw pillow off the end of the sofa and hugged it to her. "Much stronger, considering the reason you're here."

Finally, he stepped into the office. Stepped in, shut the door behind him and threw the entire room into darkness. It took her eyes several seconds to adjust and find him, and when she did he was still on the opposite side of the office, standing with his back to the door.

"I think you should go now, Michael. You can stay in my cabin tonight, and if you choose to remain in Elkhorn beyond tomorrow, we'll find you someplace else."

"You really can't understand that all I want to do is protect her, can you?"

"From Dimitri, no, I can't."

Michael walked across the room, his footsteps quiet, and paused at the edge of the sofa for a moment, as if weighing his next move. Then he sat down next to her. They were miles apart yet so very close. Closer than she wanted to be, so she pulled further to the end to make sure there was no chance of an unintentional touch of the arms, brush of the thighs. In spite of the anger she was fighting royally to hold on to, what she was feeling right now was anything but anger, and it frightened her because for all her vast inexperience in matters such as this, she knew exactly what it was. And the fact that everything inside her seemed to be betraying her right then made matters worse. "Michael, no…" This was getting too personal, and the one thing she would not be with him was personal.

"No, what? You don't want to have a civilized chat over this?"

"It's not our matter to discuss."

"She wrote him another check, Alek. I'm on her account as a secondary, which makes it my matter to discuss."

"And what has she said about it? Did you ask her why? Or is it easier to fling accusations without knowing?" Had there been another inch in which to scoot she would have, but short of getting up there was no place left to go. And she wouldn't give up her spot to him for any reason.

"She said that it's none of my business, that it's

her money to do with as she sees fit. And my mother has never been a secretive woman, Alek. Never! Except about this."

"If that's what she says, then it isn't any of your business. And she's right. It is her money." She understood his protectiveness, but that didn't alter the facts. Dimitri was not involved in anything wrong. "You've got to understand that I'm more than Dimitri's partner, and I'll do whatever it takes to watch after someone I love."

"Well, someone you love is interfering with someone I love and I'm not going to allow anything to happen to her, which puts us at an impasse, doesn't it? Two people, opposite interests, same need to protect. So where do we go from here?"

A sharp rap at the door ended the debate, and Mariska didn't wait for Alek to answer before she opened the door and stepped in. "We have an emergency up at Ridgeover, Alek, and they can't get him in to us in time."

"Who?" she asked, jumping up from the sofa, glad for any excuse to get away from Michael.

"Bill Waite. They brought him in on the boat from Almick Island complaining of a bellyache, but Oolagon Rock had a look at him and says it's appendicitis, and he thinks it might even be close to perforating."

"Temperature?"

"Elevated, but they don't have a thermometer."

"Tender to the touch?"

"Oolagon says Bill is screaming like a woman giving birth. Oh, and they're snowed in pretty well. But the landing strip is clear, and they're setting out torches right now."

"Okay, call Dimitri and tell him I'm going north. I was taking on-call, but one of them is going to have to do that. And get my surgical kit ready. I'm going to run home, change my clothes and head on out."

"ETA?" Mariska asked.

Alek glanced at her watch. "Once I get home I've got to call the weather service so, depending on what they say, forty-five minutes, give or take fifteen. Oh, and tell Oolagon I'd rather have iron dogs at the landing strip. I don't like driving on his roads in a pickup truck." She laughed. "Or riding on them when he's driving. And call Walter Rasmussen and tell him to make sure I'm set to go when I get there."

"Already did," Mariska said, "and he's pretty grumpy about being interrupted at this time of the night, but he said he'll have her out and warmed up for you, and you know what it's going to cost you."

Alek nodded. She trusted Walter with her Cessna like she trusted nobody else. He was a bit of a good-natured grump about it every time she asked him to get her plane ready to go, but he calmed right down with the promise of gouryevskaya kasha—a favorite Russian fruit dessert. One of Alek's specialties.

"And he shall have his gouryevskaya kasha as soon as I get back. Which he already knows. Oh, and give me a good stock of—"

"I know," Mariska said, sounding a bit peevish. "Antibiotics, pain meds… I've been doing this right here in this very clinic since you were in diapers, young lady. Remember? In fact, I'm the one who taught you how to prepare for an outbound."

Grabbing up her medical bag, Alek headed out the door, gave Mariska a quick kiss on the cheek, then motioned for Michael to follow. "Don't just stand there, city boy. This is wilderness medicine at its best. You wouldn't want to miss it, would you?" Probably a dumb thing to do, asking him to come along. But two medical heads and four medical hands during an appendectomy were always better. And any reason to keep him away from Dimitri until she could figure out what to do was welcome. Even if they did have to sit shoulder-to-shoulder in the cabin of the plane and would probably fight every kilometer of the way.

"I'm not quite sure I'm connecting the words 'landing strip' with 'house call', which is what we're about to do, isn't it? Fly to a house call?"

"Yep. We're flying," Alek called back as she ran to the front door of the clinic.

"And this Walter who wants gouryevskaya kasha is flying us?"

"You don't need Dramamine, do you?" she asked as she reached the sidewalk. "It can get a little choppy."

"No, I don't need Dramamine," he returned, running to catch up to her.

"Well, don't say that I didn't warn you, because it's going to be rough on touchdown since we're using an open field, not a runway."

"An open field?"

"In a valley, between the mountains. It's done like that all the time up here, city boy. You take any solid, clear landing you can get. Ice, snow, water, and sometimes, if you're lucky, land."

"And Walter won't have a problem with that, right?"

Alek laughed aloud as she waved to Dimitri, who stepped out onto his front porch at the precise moment she was passing his house. "I wouldn't trust Walter two feet off the ground, let alone in a landing of any sort. He's half-blind. Diabetic retinopathy. Good flyboy in his day, though."

"And yet you're letting him fly us?"

"No, I'm flying us. I'm the pilot, Michael. Have been for years." Nearly ten years, actually. "Walter was my instructor, though."

Michael stopped dead on the sidewalk as Alek scooted up the walk to Dimitri's cabin. "I'm taking him with me," she said to Dimitri, then laughed. "I think. Although he's looking pretty queasy about it,"

"I called the weather service for you, and by the time you get to the plane I'll have a flight plan put in for you, too. So you're good to go."

"I'd be glad to dump Michael and take you

along, if you want," she said sympathetically. Dimitri had been the pilot until a year ago, when he'd failed the vision test, and she knew it bothered him that he couldn't make these calls any longer. At least, not as the pilot. "Maggie can cover, and that idiot son of hers can help if she needs it. It could be really good, Dimitri, just the two of us again. And I know Oolagon would love to see you." Oolagon was a healer of sorts. In actuality, he was a retired engineer who'd spent years in an oil refinery then returned to his home for an easier life, which was looking after the people on the northern end of the peninsula. He'd taken basic medic training from Dimitri, which was a blessing because Ridgeover, which sat on the other side of the line demarcating the Arctic Circle, and so many other areas up there were almost cut off from everything during the winter months.

"I think you need to get there faster than I can travel now," Dimitri said.

"I'm going in on an iron dog," she said, trying to tempt him, because Dimitri did love a good ride on a snow machine.

"And I was planning on hitching up your

dogsled team and giving Maggie a run about the area tomorrow," he said. "Which is better than going off for an appendectomy, although I'm sure you don't believe that."

"One more crack about my dull life and I might forget how to make oladi."

He clutched playfully at his heart. "Not that!"

Laughing, Alek blew him a goodbye kiss. "See you tomorrow, or the day after, depending on how things go."

"And you be careful. That man seems to be giving you the eye."

"You can't see that in the dark," she said, then took a quick look at Michael and laughed. "I think he's debating the merits of Dramamine versus a brown paper bag."

"Call me from Walter's," Dimitri yelled as Alek sprinted back out to the sidewalk. "I'll have the latest forecast ready for you."

She didn't wait for Michael to catch up to her this time. Instead, she jogged across the street and over to her own cabin, then went straight inside.

"You were in my bed?" she snapped, as Michael finally stepped inside.

"Technically, no." He laughed. "But I was

curious about that lovely scent of lavender I kept smelling."

"So you were in my bedroom!"

"Lavender suits you, Alek. I think jasmine might suit you better, though. It's a little bolder. Has a little more kick to it. Lavender is subdued and polite. So you might think about jasmine."

She shook her head, wondering if dragging him along was the smart thing to do. "I don't have time for this," she said, pointing to his parka. "Grab that and your boots and let's get out of here."

"You're assuming I'm really going to fly with you?"

"I'm assuming that you're everything you taught me to be. If that's the case, then you can't stay behind because no good wilderness doctor would. But it's your choice. I can do this with or without you." Her lips turned up into a slight grin. "And if you stay behind, I'm locking my bedroom."

For whatever odd reason she couldn't define, she wanted him to go with her, which scared her more than the crazy thoughts whirling around her head, because those were only thoughts and this was reality. A great big, fuzzy reality that didn't make any sense.

Yet it made so much sense.

CHAPTER EIGHT

"YOU can look now," Alek said to Michael as she settled back in her seat now that they were up and on their way.

"Look at what? It's dark down there." He was clutching the edges of the leather seat like a panicked goose, hoping she didn't notice that his knuckles were white. Airplanes were meant to be huge—two pilots, several cabin attendants, little bottles of alcohol served to calm fidgety nerves, stale pretzels in foil bags, three hundred other people in roughly the same high-strung condition flying along for good measure. What in the world had possessed him to come with her, anyway?

"I have an instruments rating," she said, then laughed. "So you don't have to worry because most likely we won't get lost. And I think Walter probably gave us a full tank of gas so chances are we're not going to get stranded out there tempting fate by hoping that some kind person passes by who can lead us to the next filling station."

He shot her a less-than-amused look, and as the plane hit a little dip, he sat up rigidly in his seat. "You're really enjoying this, aren't you? Holding me captive in this tin can so you can taunt and torture me."

"Actually, yes, I am. It's the most fun I've had in days."

"Should I have asked to see your license before coming up with you?" he asked, trying to sound light about it, even though he was anything but.

"License?" she teased. "They require a license for this?"

"Okay, so you've got the best of me. I don't like small planes. Does it make you happy to hear me admit that? I'll fly on a regular airplane, but I hate these little things."

"Yes," she said. "It makes me happy to hear you admit it. Confession is good for the soul, you know. It reduces you to the level of the rest of us mere mortals."

"You're evil, Alek Sokolov. Pure evil."

Smiling, she gave the plane another little dip—

this one on purpose—then glanced over at him. "Don't look now, but your hair is standing on end."

"Evil, and *not* funny," he snarled through gritted teeth. "So how long are you going to get to torture me?"

"A little over half an hour. Not nearly long enough, but we've got the wind with us, so this is just a short hop over the mountain." She frowned. "You don't have panic attacks, do you?"

"No." He glared at her. "I don't have panic attacks."

"Good, because I'd hate to have to make you crawl over the seat and sit in the back. It can get a little turbulent back there on the floor."

He took a glance over his shoulder. The back was set up for medical transport, with a fold-up stretcher, oxygen cylinder, and a portable defibrillator. All things considered, it was a nice little rig. Which would have been nicer sitting stationary on the ground. "So, how often do you go out on a call like this?"

"Oh, I do an outbound maybe three or four times a month. More in the winter than the summer, since travel is difficult."

"And Dimitri doesn't go with you?"

"We rarely ever went together when he could fly because someone had to stay behind at the clinic. When Olga was alive... Olga was his wife, she often went along. Then after she died, the state sent medical staffers in for short-term assignments until I came home to take over the practice, and through that time Dimitri was the only one to go out.

"I think Walter used to fly along with him if it was going to be a rough trip and he needed a second. He'd had some medic training in the army. But Dimitri lost his license last year, so now it's all up to me. I go, and sometimes take one of the nurses or volunteers. And having your mother here is going to be a huge help, Michael, because there will be another doctor to go along now while someone stays back." And before the words were out, she instantly regretted them.

"No way in hell are you bringing my mother up here!"

"Do you stand over her during surgery and tell her how to make an incision or tie a suture?"

"Not if she's on flat ground I don't."

"You honestly think I'm a bad pilot, don't you?" Alek snapped. "I forgave you for calling me a bad doctor years ago, but now you're calling me a horrible pilot."

"I honestly don't know what kind of pilot you are. But I sure as hell don't want you piloting my mother about. Which is one more reason for me to get her out of here."

"Here's a hint, Michael. I'm still here, in one piece. That should tell you how good a pilot I am. And the fact that about a year ago we—as in Dimitri and me, the people of all the villages we attend, and the Alaskan government—invested a small fortune, more money than I'll probably make in my entire life, to buy this particular airplane to get us from place to place, should tell you that this is a very needed service up here and I'm pretty good at providing it, including the part where I have to fly to it."

"I'm not faulting anything about you or your medical practice. Probably more than most, I do know how badly the services are needed. But not my mother's services, Alek. Money aside, she needs to come home."

"Why, Michael? Why does she need to go home when she's happy here? More than that, why does she need to go someplace where she can't practice her medicine when she's needed here? Why would you want to take all that away from her?"

"It's not a matter of taking anything away," he said, then settled back in the seat and shut his eyes. "It's a matter of restoring things to the way they should be." Maybe he owed Alek an explanation for that, too. Certainly, she would think that if she knew the rest. But how could you tell someone that in the darkest hours of your life you'd failed the people who meant the most to you? "So when we get to Ridgeover and take the dogsled, then what? Surgery in an igloo?"

"First, we're not dogsledding. That's a fun way to get around, but we're going in by iron dog, which to you, city boy, is a snowmobile or snow machine, whatever you want to call it. It's fast, efficient, and takes far less upkeep than the dogs. As for the igloo situation, personally I prefer my surgeries in a little warmer structure than that. Igloos are more of a tourist illusion now. They are ice huts that are still used for protection basically—for hunters, fishermen—but not homes where people live. Up here in Alaska we've actually progressed to this odd anomaly called a house." She smiled at him. "But if you'd like, while I'm doing the appendectomy, I can have somebody show you how to make an igloo so you'll have a place to spend the night."

"I prefer to sleep in a room that's above freezing," he said. "Something with room service is nice, too."

"Because you're spoiled."

"I'll admit that," he said, relieved to be off the subject of his mother. "Spoiled, and glad to be."

"Since you like the easy life, why wilderness medicine as a subspecialty? I can see you being in trauma, heading an emergency department. But that's a different world than wilderness practice, yet that's what you teach. I guess what I'm asking is why you practice one thing and teach another."

"Because someone needs to get it right out in the wilderness. If they don't, people die for needless reasons. Running an emergency in the wilderness isn't the same as running one in the emergency room, but so many people assume that it is. Even experienced trauma physicians. I started looking into procedures purely for my own benefit, saw the lack of training, and eventually started teaching. Then it became a passion of mine"

"One you don't practice?" she asked.

He shrugged. "I have my emergency department."

"And you like that more than wilderness?"

"I like it differently, which probably sounds a little odd, but I don't know how else to describe it. It's what I do, what I was trained to do, and with teaching wilderness medicine I get the best of both my worlds."

"That explains it, but you don't sound so convincing."

"Don't have to sound convincing. It is what it is."

"Well, since I don't have to be convinced, tell me how this passion for wilderness medicine came to be."

Another story he'd never told anyone. He was laying open a vein and letting it all bleed out for Alek tonight. Funny thing was, he didn't mind doing it. "I was still a medical student the first time I saw a medical disaster resulting from poor treatment in wilderness practice. It was a simple case of frostbite and a pair of too-tight boots. Up until then, even though the educated part of me knew better, I thought you could simply shake frostbite off, keep the extremities moving, then submerge them in warm water. But after what I saw… The doctor in the field had done just about everything wrong. Not intentionally, of course. But all the adjuncts to field therapy were wrong. He used radiant warmth trying to rewarm the poor guy's feet—heat from the campfire, if you can imagine that. He didn't put gauze between the toes and the poor bastard macerated." The skin literally grew so thin it stuck together and ripped at the slightest movement. "Then the doctor kept tight socks on his feet because he thought they would be warm. If there had been a how-not-to book written on frostbite, I'd have sworn the doc would have had it in his hip pocket. So when they finally got the patient to us…gangrenous necrosis." The leg tissue had literally died. "He lost his legs and he was damned lucky he didn't lose his life.

"It was a rude awakening for me because field treatment should have been straightforward, but the doctor didn't know how and even though he used his best judgment, it wasn't good enough. He wasn't experienced in wilderness medicine and he was doing the best he could. So I decided that even though I wasn't going to practice it—

I was too far into my trauma residency to turn back—I wanted to teach it to make sure the wilderness patients who got to me had been treated right. Most likely that patient would have lost his feet no matter what anybody did, since he was third-degree frostbite to begin with, but I decided that somebody had to go beyond what they teach in medical school, especially when I remembered what the poor patient suffered."

"I think that's a very noble cause," she said. "And a worthy one. Too bad you don't practice what you preach because you've got such excitement in your voice when you talk about it. Dimitri and I get greenhorns coming through the clinic from time to time—doctors who think they know how to run a practice like ours and for whatever reason want to come up and spend a few weeks observing and working. Some of them are anxious to learn, others think they know it all. Some do know, most don't, and those are the ones who become disappointed when we don't let them haul out to an avalanche or an emergency appendectomy on a remote island in the middle of the night. It's a different medical world, and some can do it, but most cannot. And it's a true passion, otherwise nobody would do it because it's so difficult."

"And my mother? She's not experienced in it."

"I don't know your mother, and I haven't seen her work as a physician. But Dimitri's impressed, and it has nothing to do with her money. She could have all the money in the world and if she wasn't the kind of doctor who would fit in well here, and one who could work the way we need to, he wouldn't allow it. It's as simple as that."

"But you're trusting me right now."

"I'm trusting that you're as good as your reputation. If you're not, I always have an opening for someone to clean up after me. Mop up, put away, that kind of thing. So are you, Doctor? Are you as good as your reputation?"

He chuckled. "I have my moments." Why was he doing this? Why was he telling her so many things? He twisted to look out the window. Maybe because it was a good way to keep his mind off the fact that he was up in an airplane in the middle of the night with a woman who probably wouldn't think twice about dumping him out the door, without a parachute.

Or maybe it was because he actually felt comfortable with her.

In the moments when she wasn't absolutely despising him, he caught himself thinking how much he liked her, in spite of the way they seemed to go at each other. But, then, maybe that was part of what he liked.

"I suppose we all have our moments, don't we?" she said, sighing. "And I'm sorry about being so grumpy with you all the time. But you've got to understand—"

"Actually, I do. You're protecting someone, like I am."

"Neither of whom need, or want, protecting," she said, then laughed. "And right now they're plotting some way to end our interference, which is exactly what we'd be doing if the situation was reversed."

"Ah, but isn't it our sworn duty to interfere in the lives of those we love?" If he'd interfered more in his father's life, Eric Morse might still be alive. But he hadn't taken the time to notice, or to even support his mother when she did. A two-year battle with prostate cancer—one that might have had another outcome but for the lack of interference from someone who should have interfered, someone who had been caught up in his own disconsolate world.

"I try every chance I get. It's probably a good thing I don't love too many people, isn't it?"

"Yes," he said quite soberly.

Alek glanced sideways at him. "Since we were actually having few nice moments, I thought you might protest that a little."

"See how you are? I agreed totally with you, and you expect me to argue. I can't win with you, can I?"

"No," she said quite soberly, then they both laughed.

"So I'm curious. Why bother taking your wilderness certification when you live the life? It's not required by law. And I'm betting you could probably teach the class as well as I do."

"Better," she said lightly. "Instead of lecturing, I would have brought the class up here and put them through some practical experience. Nothing beats book learning better than good, hands-on practice, and Dimitri and I usually have plenty of that to go around."

"So, like I said, why the class?"

"Dimitri insisted. He said it was for the prestige of the clinic but I think it was because he likes for me to get out of here every now and then."

"Because it's so isolated?"

"No, I love the isolation, and we have everything here you could possibly want. Warm climates, cold climates, long days, long nights. And the countryside…beaches, ice fields, forests. We have hundreds of varieties of flowers and even though the season is short, when they come alive…there's nothing like it anyplace in the world. And the animal populations… Where else can you have bears, caribou, moose, walruses, oxen, eagles, reindeer and whales? But most of all the people are the best. It's such an exciting mix of indigenous Alaskans, Russians and people from everywhere else who can't pass up the lure of the wilds. And we wouldn't have any of this if we weren't isolated and separated from the lower forty-eight, because people would overrun us, trying to get here.

"So being isolated isn't why Dimitri sent me off for certification. I think he wanted me to snare a husband. That's been on his mind a lot lately. He's afraid I'm about to pass my prime. I also think he wants grandsons. Maybe a grand-daughter or two, since he's awfully good with little girls."

"I didn't think he was your—"

"He's not. Long story."

And she wasn't going into it. The set look on her face told him the topic was off-limits and the last thing he was about to do was stress the pilot of his plane. "I'm wounded. You took my class because you were husband-hunting and not because you wanted to listen to my brilliant teaching style."

"Dimitri was husband-hunting. I was taking your class because you do have a good reputation and I wanted to hear what you had to say."

"And you challenged me from your dark little hidey-hole in the back row so eloquently. Every chance you got."

"Only when you needed it."

"So, did you learn anything at all, other than the fact that your instructor was a complete jackass?"

"Only that I loved my wilderness practice more than I'd realized, and I missed it dreadfully while I was away. Oh, and he wasn't a complete jackass. At least, not all the time. And I did appreciate your lectures on West Nile virus since in all likelihood, with the huge mosquito population we already have in Alaska, we'll have it introduced here in the not-too-distant future."

"Are you trying to be kind to me?"

"Why would I want to be kind?" She chuckled. "Especially now that you're trapped and can't get away?"

"Like I said, you're evil."

"And if you don't quit gripping the armrests like that, you're going to have muscle spasms in your hands. Which won't do me any good in surgery."

He glanced down, then immediately relaxed his grip and wiggled his fingers to restore the circulation to them. "I don't suppose I could catch a bus or train back to Elkhorn when we're through, could I?"

Alek dipped the plane and pointed out the window to the array of lights on the ground. "Our destination. Now all I have to do is manage to land between the rows of light."

"And if you don't?"

"Well, we have several options then. Trees, a mountain, the torch fires. If I overshoot by much, the Kotzebue Sound. All rather inhospitable."

He studied Alek's face for a moment, and saw the smile tugging at the corners of her mouth before he closed his eyes for the landing. Instead of grabbing hold of the armrests again, he merely folded his hands in his lap. "You're good," he said.

"At what?"

A great many things, he suspected. In her element, Alek was spectacular. "Getting my mind off the fact that you've held my life in the palm of your hand for the past half hour, and you're landing me safely in spite of the fact that you hate me."

"Hate's such a strong word. I think despise will do quite nicely, though."

Michael opened his eyes at the instant the wheels made contact with the ground, and he chanced a quick look at Alek.

She was smiling at him, and that's when it hit him. "Damn," he grunted, shaking his head. How could this be happening? And with her, of all people? Maybe it was merely the effect of a lonely man being too close to a gorgeous woman for too long. Somehow, though, he didn't think so. It might not be love in the complete sense, but he sure could be sneaking up on something like it. Affection, fondness, attraction… "Damn," he muttered again.

"Are you swearing because it was that good or that bad?"

"Don't know yet," he muttered. "I really don't know."

He was actually kind of cute, sitting there all panic-stricken and white-knuckled. It hadn't been a bad trip overall. They'd gotten along quite nicely, and if not for that one big wedge still between them, she might have even fancied him a friend. Of course, that was going too far because she still knew why he was there. "So have you ever been on an iron dog?" she asked as she opened her door. "Because we've got another ten kilometers to cover, and you can have your choice, front or back." The idea of sitting behind, clinging to him, did have a rather nice appeal to it. As silly as it might seem, she was keeping her fingers crossed that he did have snowmobiling experience because him sitting behind her, holding on, wasn't nearly as exciting as her holding on to him. And straddling that iron dog behind Michael did evoke a feeling or two.

"I'm surprised you'd trust me to get you there."

"Oh, I don't trust you that much. But Oolagon will lead the way." She pointed to a remote figure standing off to the side of the landing area—a large man, with long, gray hair tied back into a ponytail, and a somber look on his face. He was swinging a lantern back and forth as a signal. "And he'll be pretty good to lead you around the occasional moose that might have stepped out into the path."

Michael reached back over the seat to pull out the various bags and boxes of supplies, and one by one handed them out to Alek. "Since you were in charge in the plane, I'll be in charge on the iron dog. My turn to torture you."

"Absolutely. Anything you want to say, or anything you want to do, as long as it doesn't end with me on the ground."

"Coming from you, that offer's hard to refuse."

"But you've driven one, haven't you?" she asked, handing two of her packs to one of the men who'd helped set up the torch field. "This won't be your first time?"

"You think I'm a beginner on the iron dog?" A devious chuckle rumbled from his chest. "I suppose you'll have to wait and see, won't you?" Michael hopped out, exchanged greetings with the man who was there to help, then headed over to the iron dog and climbed on. "You're lagging behind, Alek," he called. "Everybody's waiting for you."

Suddenly, she didn't know if this was such a bright idea after all. A good case of fantasy over practicality, and now she was beginning to regret it. But he'd already taken his place in the snow-mobile queue, right behind Oolagon and in front of the other men, and they were waiting for her to come on board. If she didn't hurry, well, she knew how people were about Michael. They'd take him on ahead to Bill Waite, then return for her when it was convenient. "On my way," she called, running over to the line and hopping on behind him.

After fastening on her helmet, she snaked her arms around his waist then laid her cheek on his back—on the cold fur of his parka. In spite of the brisk temperature, she felt a spark of heat. His or hers? She didn't know, but the instant her arms reached around him she felt it, and it was enough to keep her warm. Enough, actually, to make her sweat inside her parka. A nice warmth and not so much about staving off the cold as it was about the proximity to Michael. And she liked that far more than she should. "I can do this," she shouted as he revved the engine. "I can drive."

"You gave me my choice," he shouted back. "Now, hold on tight because I don't go back for anyone who bumps off."

He didn't have to ask her twice to hold on tight. She'd been this route before and knew all the bumps intimately. Of course, there was a new little bump tonight—the one bumping double-speed in her chest—and she knew it wasn't about the impending ride. Not in the least.

So she was falling for him? What of it? In another day or two he'd be gone, and she'd get over him like she had the first time she'd had a little infatuation. Of course, the first time, she hadn't got quite this close, and he'd certainly put an end to her feelings—albeit feelings from afar—in an ugly way. Now, even through the thickness of all their many layers of clothing, this closeness was nice in a way she hadn't expected. Impossible, but nice. And, yes, to answer her own question, she was falling for him all over again, as stupid as that was. They had obstacles, they had issues, but none of that was sinking through the outer layers and convincing her heart to slow down.

"Really stupid," she said, as he accelerated. "Nothing good's going to come of it." Except the ride, which was very good pressed so tight against him, and she did love the way her body fit so well to his, even through all the padding.

The ride to Ridgeover was much quicker than she expected, and Michael was proficient in his snowmobile skills. Except for a couple of good hard smacks along the way, the trip was surprisingly smooth. As she climbed off when they came to a stop outside a well-lit wooden cabin on the edge of Ridgeover, a village of substantially less than a hundred people, it didn't take her long at all to find her land legs and scurry up the wooden steps and inside. Ahead of Michael for once. She was still flushed, which she didn't want him to see, and it wasn't from the ride.

"Bill?" she said, dropping her parka on the floor next to the door. "It's Alek Sokolov. I'm here with Dr. Morse, and we're going to take care of you." She didn't know Bill Waite. To her recollection she'd never met him, and when she saw the large, lumberjack-looking man lying on the bed, red as a bowl of her best borscht and sweating like he was in a sauna, she was immediately concerned that his appendix had already burst.

"Appreciate that, Doc," he panted, trying to smile up at her from his supine position. "Hurts like hell, pardon my language."

"I'll bet it does. No need to apologize. How long has it been hurting?"

"Three, four days, off and on. Not too bad until this afternoon, then it felt like all hell broke loose inside."

Alek took his wrist to check his pulse. Elevated. Not as strong as she would have liked. Then she watched the rise and fall of his chest to measure his respirations. Fast and shallow. And from the feel of his face, she was betting on a temperature a good four to five degrees above normal. As soon as Michael and Oolagon came in with the medical supplies, she'd check it with a thermometer. "Okay. I'm going to do a little prodding on your belly. Tell me when it only hurts, and when it hurts like hell." As if she didn't already know.

Alek took a quick look at the woman who'd been attending Bill Waite. She was called Umuk, although Alek didn't know her last name. "Has he had anything for pain?" she asked. "An aspirin, an ibuprofen? Any kind of a local cure?" And the people here did use local remedies of berries and roots and bark, and even animal fat. She smiled grimly. Michael's quackery come to pass. Out here it was all around him.

Umuk shook her head. "Oolagon said no, that we needed to keep him clean. So he's had nothing. Not even water."

Alek smiled. "Good. Now, would you mind getting me a bucket of snow?" The best cooling agent for the surgery, and she had an unlimited supply right outside the door.

Umuk nodded, then scurried away as Alek pulled the covers back from Bill's chest, unzipped the flannel-lined jeans he was wearing and began her examination. She started her probing high, to see how far the pain radiated. "Just let me know," she told him.

"Believe me, Doc, that's what I've been doing for hours, letting everybody within shouting distance know."

There wasn't significant pain anywhere on the left side of his abdomen, but once she ventured over to the right and began to work her way downward, his barely audible gasps went to quiet moans and then to loud moans. By the time she'd reached the lower right quadrant, his moans turned into screams, and without the benefit of any modern testing equipment, she knew she had her culprit. A mighty hot appendix. Whether or not it had perforated, sending the infecting poisons out through his system, remained to be seen. She hoped not, but if she were a betting woman, she would have bet on it.

Michael flew in the door at approximately the same time Bill quit screaming, and dropped the bags of medical supplies on the floor next to Alek's parka. "What's the verdict?" he asked, sliding out of his outerwear and letting it fall into the pile with the rest.

"Red hot and ready to go, I'd say. And no time to waste."

"Has it perforated?"

She stepped over to the door out of Bill's earshot. "Probably. And I don't think taking him back for the surgery is a good idea because right now he's in no condition for a ride out the way we rode in. It would probably kill him."

"So we do it here."

He sounded casual about it, and a simple appendectomy wouldn't have been such a worry. But if this one had burst, cabin surgery put him at risk almost as much as taking him back to the hospital. Either way, there wasn't a good option here. Bill was in for a rough go no matter what they did. "I don't see another choice. It would be easier if all we had to do was snip it, but he's awfully sick and this has been going on for days. So if the appendix hasn't burst yet, it's awfully close, and I don't think we should let it go on any longer. And, Michael, so you'll know, I'm glad you're here."

Michael bent down and when Alek expected him to whisper something to her, he gave her a gentle kiss on the lips. Short, sweet and, oh, so unexpected.

"So am I, Alek," he said quietly. Then he gave her another kiss, a little bolder, a little longer. Deep, arousing. A little more puzzling. "So am I."

CHAPTER NINE

"No whiskey this time," Alek teased Michael as she tied on her surgical mask. "It may be fine for yanking out a tooth, but not for an appendix."

"Not even for the anesthetist?" he asked, a wide grin crossing his face as he checked the IV drip going into Bill. The bag of fluids was hanging from a moose head suspended over the bed—hooked on to one of the antlers. And Oolagon was busy dragging every last light in the cabin into place around the bed.

Alek glanced up at the moose head, saw a surgical mask placed over its nose, and laughed. "From the looks of this surgery you've set up, I'd say you already found the whiskey. You and your buddy on the wall up there."

"You ought to laugh more often," he said. "You get the cutest little crinkle around your eyes."

She was glad the mask covered all but her eyes

because she could feel a warm blush creep across her cheeks and she didn't want him to know he'd caused it, because he would, invariably, read more into it than there was. One little kiss, or actually two, and a nice compliment did not a relationship make, and right now she had the blush of a woman who might be falling in love. Or maybe had fallen a while ago and was only now beginning to realize it. But that woman couldn't be her—not with him. And it wasn't because of Dimitri, since once that whole situation was on the table for everybody to examine, he would see that Dimitri wasn't at all what he thought him to be. It was two different worlds colliding, and hers was too set to change. She didn't know how to begin even if she wanted to.

Somehow, the splendid isolation of Alaska seemed to smile on that decision. Although Alaska didn't share her bed at night, and it did get lonely. But it was the price she was reconciled to pay because it was simply...easier. Alaska wouldn't turn its back on her. Neither would Dimitri. Those were her only guarantees in life.

So Alek was glad to hide behind the mask and not let Michael see how he was affecting her. "Is our patient ready?" she asked, glancing back up at the moose. "You've checked his vitals again, and talked to him about allergies?"

"His vitals are the same as they were earlier, except his temperature, which is gradually creeping up. And he denied allergies to anything—no medications, no foods, although moose does give him a little indigestion." He glanced up at the moose head, too. "So I started the drip and by now he's sleeping like a baby. One little dose of ketamine along with a lullaby and he's good to go." Michael pulled on his own mask and tied it behind his head. "And don't think I didn't see you blush, Alek, because I did."

"Did not," she argued. "Because I don't blush."

"Then maybe I should take your temperature before we start, because you might have a fever." He glanced at his watch. Timing was everything and they still had a few minutes to wait until the drugs took complete hold.

"Just the effects of the moment. That's all."

"And maybe a kiss?"

"Are you running a prophylactic drug for the infection?" she blurted, trying to get off the subject.

"Two in combination. I found ceftizoxime and

cefotetan in your kit so I hung both of them since we don't know what kind of bug we're fighting. And are you trying to avoid what happened, Alek? Trying to avoid talking about it?"

"Something for nausea?" she persisted, still trying not to be drawn into a personal conversation. "Because once he wakes up I don't want him to—"

"I gave him ondansetron," Michael interrupted, taking several steps closer to her. "He'll be fine when he wakes up. Better than you, probably. At least, not as evasive." Then he bent low to her ear. "It's not over, Alek." Making sure that Oolagon was watching over their patient, Michael pulled Alek into the bedroom. "You can evade all you want, but it's not over."

"I'm not being evasive, Michael. I'm trying to concentrate. And there's nothing started to be over with. You got carried away…"

"You haven't seen me yet when I'm carried away."

"Why are you doing this?" she hissed. "Especially now, when I should be focusing on what I'm about to do." Truth was, the surgery wasn't making her in the least nervous, but he was because she was afraid she had no will to resist him. Attraction aside, these past couple of days had made her realize that in all his various moods and manifestations, she hadn't gotten over her very first reaction to him that day he'd walked onto the lecture stage. The tiff over Dimitri was a good excuse to put him at arm's length, but eventually that tiff would be solved. Then what?

Iron will. That's what. Especially if Maggie were to stay with Dimitri, because that meant Michael would always thread in and out of her life in some way. And she was going to have to be the one to give him the straight arm—and never, ever bend it. "I really need to think about the procedure," she lied, backing away from him.

"It's a three-inch incision, Alek. You could do it in your sleep. I think you're trying *not* to concentrate on something that has nothing to do with an appendectomy." He stepped to the door and looked out at Oolagon, who was monitoring Bill's vital signs. Oolagon gave him the thumbs-up sign.

"Okay, you want to talk about it, we'll talk. What's there to say, Michael? You kissed me. I've been kissed before." But never like that.

Even in its brevity, it had almost buckled her knees. Without any romantic intent whatsoever, it had been a kiss like she'd never imagined—the one she'd read about in all the romance novels that sizzled, and burned her lips and lingered. "People do strange things in tense situations, and it's not a big deal."

"And you think me kissing you was a strange thing?"

"Do you honestly think that this...this... whatever it is you're toying with between us could work, Michael? A flirtation, an affair? First of all, there's distance, and I have no intention of trying to close the geographical gap between us. I'm staying right where I am. And then, in case you've forgotten, there's the reason you came to Alaska—to snatch your mother out of Dimitri's depraved grasp. And I'm warning you again, like I have before, that I'll never, ever let you hurt Dimitri in any way. So after we wade through all of that, do you still honestly believe that what you're trying to start is wise? Or maybe you've turned me into your lost holiday—go to Alaska, find a woman who hasn't been with a man, and in her desperation she'll succumb to your charms, fall into your bed and salvage what's left of your holiday." She drew in a deep, steadying breath. "Not now, Michael. I won't do this now. I'm here to be a doctor, and if you're not…"

Instead of answering, arguing or otherwise coming back at her, which she expected and most likely deserved, Michael merely pulled his mask down, took several steps forward and gave Alek a tender kiss on the forehead. Then he pulled his mask back up, glanced at his watch again and said, "Before we start our next battle, I'd suggest we start the appendectomy first."

No more words between them, no more animosities, which were pretty one-sided, anyway. He was right. It was time to operate. Alek glanced up at the moose as she took her place at the makeshift operating table directly underneath its head. It was looking directly at Michael. But of course it was!

"Damn," Michael muttered as he adjusted the IV drip. "I was really hoping it hadn't perforated. Now we don't have a choice. He's going to have to go back to Elkhorn with us."

"It could have been worse," Alek said. She was

irrigating the infected area, trying to clean it out. "I'm not seeing nearly as much infection in here as I thought there might be, so I don't think he's been this sick for as long as we thought he was." She glanced over the top of her surgical mask at Michael. "But I was hoping I'd made the wrong diagnosis and that the appendix hadn't perforated. It would have been easier leaving him here for his recovery."

"Just goes to show you're a damn good doctor." His eyes smiled at her over the top of his mask. "No matter what some idiot doctor said about you a long time ago."

"Just goes to show you're a good judge of talent," she responded, then laughed.

"Like I said earlier, I like that little crinkle around your eyes so much better than the frown. Even through the goggles." Required protective wear for surgery.

"And I like a closed wound better than an open one, but unfortunately I don't think we should close him up tonight. Too much risk of spreading the infection, especially now that we've invaded it. We need to keep an access in, so let's get this thing packed up and stabilize him for now, then we can go crinkle and frown without goggles all we want to until morning."

"We're not taking him back right away?" Michael asked.

"Not while this pilot has bleary eyes. Not safe. So unless you're hiding a secret pilot's license from me, I'm going to take a little snooze before we go anywhere."

"Want me to finish up here?" he asked. "I think Oolagon and I can handle the rest." He glanced over at the man who'd served as a surgical technician throughout the appendectomy, and Oolagon nodded his consent.

"Actually, I'd love for you to finish up here." Without a speck of argument, Alek stepped back from the table, pulled off her paper gown, mask, goggles and gloves and tossed the surgical baton over to Michael. Then she went straight to the only bedroom in the cabin, shut the door behind her and collapsed flat on the bed, figuring that she'd probably toss and turn until it was time to get back up and fly home, trying to figure out that kiss—what it had meant, and why. More than that, trying to figure out her overreaction, and lingering feelings, about it—what those meant, and why. But she was wrong, because as the pleasant memory of his lips was slipping in, she slipped right off to sleep.

"He's going to be out for quite a while," Michael said to Oolagon. "Just keep an eye on his vital signs, check them every fifteen minutes." He was talking to a group of four local volunteers who'd come in to sit vigil. They were a serious, quiet group of men, all with the gravity of Bill's situation clearly etched on their faces. "And don't hesitate to come get me if you think something is wrong. *No matter what it is,*" he emphasized.

Bill was in a stable condition, but the antibiotics weren't knocking down his fever as they should, and Michael was concerned that the infection—peritonitis—had spread further than he and Alek had originally thought when they'd first cut in. Under the circumstances it was difficult to tell and difficult to diagnose. But the prognosis wasn't as good as he might have liked, all things considered. Bill had survived the surgery admirably, but overall his condition wasn't improving, and on top of that now he had an unclosed surgical wound to contend with and a long, bumpy ride ahead before he had any chance of getting the rest of the medical treatment he needed.

On top of it, Alek couldn't fly, which meant that precious hours were ticking away. But there was nothing left to do. Sit, watch, wait and pray for the best. "And come get me if he wakes up, or if his bandages soak through, or if—"

Oolagon stepped forward from behind the pack of volunteers and thrust out the palm of his hand to stop Michael. "We take care of our own," he said. "You don't have to worry."

"Point taken," he replied, then headed to the bedroom door. "Call me in two hours."

Oolagon gave him a polite nod, then turned his back to take Bill's pulse. Point taken, message received. It was time to take a nap, too.

Once he shut the bedroom door behind him, Michael stood there a moment, watching Alek sleep. She was huddled into a tight little ball, clinging fiercely to the center of the double bed. Such an amazing woman, he thought as he plodded across and sat down on the edge. Stubborn and a touch unmanageable, she demanded so much of others. And more of herself. He liked the fierce way she went about her life. For her, it was always a great march onto the battlefield with the strong determination to conquer.

And she did conquer. At least, she'd conquered him. More and more with each passing moment. And, yes, he did like that sass in her. It kept him alert, kept him waiting for the next round.

And sexy… My God! He still didn't have a lot of memory of her in class. More her attitude and challenge than her. But that was by her own design, he was coming to realize. She kept herself separated, reserved, alone. And was a virgin, if what she'd said out there was true. And there was no reason to think that it wasn't.

It all added up to an impossible situation. He couldn't have her, she didn't want him…and yet his mind was trying to tick off a way he *could* have and she *would* want. In what circumstances, he didn't know. Not that it mattered anyway, since it wouldn't work out.

Just fatigue, he decided. Because he sure hadn't slept much since he'd met her. A good night's sleep, or even a good couple of hours, would clear his head of all the foolish notions and get him back on track. He was sure of it!

Easing down on the mattress, trying not to disturb her, Michael raised his feet carefully off the floor, then settled in flat on his back. It had been a good long while since he'd slept with a woman, and certainly in the past, it had never been this way...simply sleeping. But the bed felt good, and even though he was taking pains not to wake her up, sleeping next to her felt pretty damn good, too, and that *wasn't* the fatigue talking.

"You don't really think you're going to stay there, do you?" she asked, not even opening her eyes. "In this bed, with me?"

Of course she would protest. She couldn't be Alek and not protest. "That's exactly what I'm thinking. In this bed, with you, since it's the only bed in the house."

"Take the floor," she said. "And a pillow, of course. It can get awfully hard down there without a pillow."

"It's not like you're sprawled over the entire top of this mattress, using every square inch of it," he countered, smiling in the dark. "And even if you tried, you couldn't, because there's not enough of you to sprawl."

"But I like options, and if you're in part of the space, you're limiting my options."

"Or expanding them, depending upon how you look at the situation."

"The point is, I don't want to look at any situation in bed next to me. If I did, I would have invited you to share my spare space. Which I didn't."

Michael laughed aloud. "You don't ever give an inch, do you?"

"Actually, you've taken far more than an inch already." Alek rolled over on her back and lay in the same position as Michael—flat, stiff-shouldered, hands folded across her belly, staring up at a dark ceiling. "And now I need your space."

"For what? You've already got plenty of your own."

"To get comfortable. Your space may be more comfortable than mine. Or I might wish to sleep diagonally. Or roll about occasionally."

"Well, you go ahead and make yourself comfortable anyplace you like except on my spot, because I'm not budging. Not a twitch. And now you're cutting into my sleeping time." He rolled over on his side, with his back to Alek, then pulled himself into a slight curl. "So unless you're going to sing me a lullaby or tell me a bedtime story, the next thing I want to hear from you is a snore."

Alek moved herself into the same position as Michael, only in the opposite direction, and as she pulled herself into a slight curl, their bottoms touched. "I don't snore. And I don't sing lullabies, either."

It was almost worth it, giving up his sleep for the nice little bickering, but she needed her sleep even more than he needed his, since she was the one who was going to have to fly them out of there come daybreak. So he didn't reply to that. Not one word. Instead, he concentrated on the feel of her bottom pressed to his, and wondered how it would be to sleep like that every night.

Pleasant. And absolutely aggravating, he decided a half minute later as she wiggled to find a better position, and he could feel that wiggle oh, so vividly, all the way through him. So had that been on purpose? he wondered. A little Aleksandra Sokolov torture, to keep him roused and, yes, aroused. A tempting little press of her bottom simply to taunt and frustrate him. And he was frustrated! Or was she actually settling in?

Hell, maybe he should sleep on the floor, because her close proximity was driving him crazy. That, and her way of wiggling at the right intervals. One more wiggle from her bottom to his and he would likely… She wiggled again! "Damn it, Alek, would you hold still?"

She didn't answer, but he did hear a soft little giggle from her side of the bed, and that's all it took. Flipping over, he spooned her. Pulled her back to him, formed his body to her curves, and slung his leg up over hers to keep her there. If this hadn't been a stranger's bed, with a room full of people on the other side of the door, not to mention one very sick man who needed better than a couple of cavorting physicians, this would only have been the beginning. But as Alek settled back against his body's contours, she let out an exhausted sigh, and within seconds he recognized the breathing pattern of someone deep in sleep.

It may not have been the way he would have planned their first night in bed together, but it was nice. Intimate. Cozy. Kissing Alek on the back of the neck, Michael shut his eyes and drifted along with her.

"He's still sedated," Michael shouted as Alek nosed the plane up. "I don't think he'll feel a thing."

"He didn't feel a thing all the way out to the plane, so the rest of this should be easy."

Michael pulled off his mitten and felt Bill's forehead. Much too warm, considering all the antibiotics they'd pumped into him and were still pumping, and all the snow packs they'd made to chill him. Plus, Alek had changed the dressing before they'd left. Of course, riding in the bed of an open pickup truck all that way couldn't have been easy on their patient. It wasn't easy on Alek and him, and they weren't sick.

But in spite of the difficulties, Oolagon had driven the truck, while the two of them, along with Umuk, had huddled in the back, tending their patient and trying, not too successfully, to buffer all the bumps along the way.

"Easy on him, maybe, but…" A rapid jerk that stiffened Bill's body for a second caused Michael to press his fingers to man's wrist to take a pulse, but as he did that, Bill lashed out, grabbing him by the wrist and effectively pulling him down to the floor in a position in which, if he resisted, Bill could have easily snapped his wrist. At the same time, Bill let out a bloodcurdling scream, followed by a string of profanities that would have made even the most foulmouthed person blush, and tried sitting up under the restraints, which made him even more combative and loud when he discovered he couldn't budge.

"Hold him still," Alek shouted. "When he's thrashing like that, I can't hold the plane steady."

"I'm trying," Michael shouted back, but he was still pinned down as Bill was beginning to twist his wrist. Another sharp twist and it would snap for sure.

Alek set the plane on autopilot, unfastened her harness briefly, then leaned back over the seat long enough to grab Bill by the other wrist. In that moment of surprise he lashed out at her, letting go of Michael. "And if he knocks you out, what am I suppose to do up here?" Michael shouted, as he scrambled to his knees to fasten the wrist restraints on the litter around Bill.

In the instant that Alek had taken hold of Bill

and he'd let go of Michael, Bill had whipped over on his side and grabbed her by the forearm, locking her into much the same position as he'd done with Michael. She slapped at her patient, not so much to hurt but to force him to let go. Unfortunately, his grip only tightened. Then came another round of cursing, followed by Bill's attempt to bite her hand. As he struggled against Alek, who was trying to free herself from his grip, he pulled up against his restraints so hard the veins in his neck were popping out and his face went a dark, angry red. "Get him restrained," she screamed at Michael over the profanity, as she pushed against Bill. "Or medicate him."

"I'm trying," Michael shouted back, as he prepared a syringe with a sedative. "But if I grab him, he's going to break your wrist."

"Better a broken wrist than a crashed plane. And he's bleeding from his wound, now," she called as the red stains from his open incision started to creep through the blanket.

To distract their patient, Michael tossed a blanket over Bill's face, and miraculously it did the trick. He immediately let go of Alek's arm and started to wrestle with the blanket, which gave

Alek enough time to fasten herself back into her seat and check her instrument readings. Wonderful plane! Her old one hadn't had an autopilot.

Once she was sure the plane was stable, Alek turned around to watch Michael swab the IV port and inject the sedative. "Is he holding on? Michael, look out!"

Too late. Bill threw off the blanket and took a swing at Michael, landing his blow square on Michael's jaw. Michael was immediately slammed backward into the side of the plane, causing a sudden shift in the aircraft balance, which caused the airplane to plunge sharply.

Alek spun back around in her seat to make corrections before the plane went into a nosedive, as Michael simply sat there on the floor, stunned and rubbing his chin. Bill continued to scream and thrash about, injuring his appendectomy wound and bleeding even more.

At this point, all Alek could do was pray for a fast effect of the sedative, try and get them home and hope for the best. "Michael?" she called over the racket. "Are you okay?"

"Okay," he called back, though he wasn't trying to get himself up.

"You need to stay where you are. Don't move. Do you hear me? Don't move. You could have a shattered jaw, neck injury or worse, and right now there's nothing I can do for you. Do you understand me, Michael? Do *not* move."

The sedative was taking over now and Bill was finally settling down. She was concerned about his bleeding but until they landed there was nothing she could do. And she certainly didn't want Michael attempting anything. "Don't move, Michael," she repeated, as Bill's screams diminished to a whimper.

"I'm fine," Michael returned.

"I'll be the judge of that once we're landed. Until then you're my patient, and I'm ordering you to keep down."

"Pretty mean punch for a sick guy," he said, sliding down to a flat position on the floor next to his patient as the cabin began to spin around him. "I think I'll be taking a nap now. Wake me up when the flight attendant comes around with those little packets of peanuts." With that, Dr. Michael Morse slipped into a deep sleep, along with his patient.

Alek looked back for a second, then turned her full attention to getting both her patients to safety.

* * *

The instant the plane rolled to a stop on the snowy landing strip, Alek was out of her harness and scrambling over the seat. She took at quick look at Michael, flashed a light in his eyes to assess pupillary action, a determining factor of potential brain damage. Once she saw that it was normal, she slipped a cervical collar around his neck then turned to Bill, who was sleeping soundly now with a contented grin on his face, of all things! Smiling in relief, she pulled back the blanket to have a look at his incision. "Now you grin at me after you almost crashed the plane." So much mess for such a small cut, but at least the bleeding had subsided, which meant it was now a matter of getting him into surgery, cleaning out his wound and sticking in a tube for a few days to make sure the infection had a good chance to drain away. She turned around and felt his head. Still too hot, but at least now he was headed off to a proper facility and not a medical make-do a hundred kilometers from nowhere.

"Looks like you've had quite a night and day

of it," Dimitri said, motioning two locals over with a stretcher.

"Surgery went well, but the ride back…" She moved aside as the attendants crawled in and lifted Bill's litter out, then set it atop the awaiting stretcher. "Let's just say that I've had better." She glanced over at Michael, and shook her head. "So has he."

"Serious?"

"Probably not. Our patient went a little wild and Michael's head got in the way."

"If you'd kept the plane level, I wouldn't have slammed into the wall," Michael commented, though his eyes were still closed.

Alek smiled at Dimitri. "Sounds to me like he's talking out of his head," she said, crawling over and sitting down next to Michael.

"And you talk in your sleep," Michael quipped, opening his eyes and raising his hand to feel the collar.

"This is something I should want to hear?" Dimitri asked, stepping back from the plane as Maggie ran up to it.

"I'm taking him to surgery," she said, looking inside. "Is Michael all right?" she asked Alek.

"As a physician, he'll survive to heal another day. As a pugilist, I think he's retired." She rubbed her fingers lightly over his jaw. It was puffy now and beginning to turn blue from bruising.

"I deserve some kind of medal for going above and beyond the call of duty," he said, struggling to sit up.

"No getting up," Alek said, pushing him gently back to a flat position. "Not until that collar comes off, and it's not coming off until we get an X-ray. Which means you get to go in on a stretcher, too, like all the other patients do."

Maggie leaned in further to take a look, and once she was satisfied her son was going to be fine, she gave him a squeeze on the arm then ran to catch up with the men hauling Bill into the back of an SUV-turned-ambulance.

"Think I'll go scrub up with her," Dimitri said, backing away, too.

"You scared him," Alek said, once the two of them were alone.

"But you do talk in your sleep." He reached up and rubbed his chin. "And you snuggle. Quite nicely, actually. Best I've had since…"

"You're loopy," she stated.

"And the best cure for that is a little tender bedside manner. Care to practice some on me?" He smiled up at her in spite of his swollen face.

"Not likely," she said, laughing.

"I'm your patient. I have needs only my doctor can take care of." He pointed to his chin. "Right there, for instance. Big need on my jaw."

"And what would cure that big need?"

He reached up and brushed his fingers across her lips. "That, for starters…"

"And you expect me to kiss you because you're playing on my sympathy?"

Rolling his eyes at her, he grinned. "Yes."

"That's forward, don't you think?"

"Yes, but it's a perfect medicine. I'm already feeling much better thinking about it." He stroked her lips again. "Much better."

How could anyone who'd been punched like that be so utterly sexy only a few minutes later? "Just one kiss?"

"Normally, these prescriptions call for much more. But one would do for starters, followed by several follow-up doses over the course of the illness."

She wanted to. Dear lord, how she wanted to, and if there had been no other considerations to be made, it would have been such an easy thing. But one would lead to another would lead to heart-break because he would leave and she wouldn't. And while he might have it in him to be cavalier about such matters, she didn't. Not at all.

Alek looked down at Michael, who'd already shut his eyes and seemed to be drifting off. "You're persuasive," she whispered. Persuasive because there was nothing she wanted to do more than give him that kiss. She always had. Always would.

Sighing, Alek gave in to her desires—for the first time in her life she allowed her heart to dictate her head, as she first ran her fingers lightly over his swollen jaw, then followed with a kiss. It was a light, delicate kiss that elicited his sigh as her lips touched him. "We shouldn't," she whispered. "Not while we don't know the extent of your injury."

"No neck injury," he said, reaching up to remove his collar. "And sometimes we have to do what we shouldn't." He raised a shaky hand to stroke her cheek. "Sometimes life has to be about the things we shouldn't do."

In her life, she'd rarely ever done what she shouldn't, and this departure, while it didn't make sense, was one of those shouldn'ts that had to happen. Every irrational impulse inside her said it had to, so she kissed him again. Light and delicate once more, as he turned his head ever so slightly, his eyes still closed, and pointed to his lips. "Right here," he whispered. "It's a little sore, too."

The kiss she placed there was much like the one to his jaw, but as she was about to pull away, Michael's hand snaked up around her neck and held her in place—her lips pressed to his—and the kiss he returned was anything but delicate and gentle. It was hard and demanding, the kiss of a lover desperate for more and not an injured man in pain. Immediately, Alek succumbed to the wild demand, returning what he was giving with a passion she'd never before known, opening her mouth to the probing of his tongue and returning his exploration with a torrential frenzy that made her realize she'd been waiting for this moment for three years.

It was only when she found herself giving more, taking more from the kiss than she should, that she pulled back from Michael. Raising her fingers to her swollen lips, the sudden impact of what had happened hit her so hard she stifled a gasp. "I'll go see what's keeping that stretcher," she choked out, then fled from the plane before he had a chance to stop her.

Outside, she leaned against the fuselage and closed her eyes, trying to forget, trying to shut it all out. But the frantic pounding of her heart wouldn't be shut out.

CHAPTER TEN

"HE'S going to be fine," Dimitri said, settling down next to Alek on the sofa in his tiny office, then pulling her into his arms. "Maggie took a look while I finished up on Bill, and it's a little contusion from the blow to the head, like we thought, but nothing's broken, nothing's permanently damaged, eyesight's fine, no diminished capacity. He'll be as good as new in a day or so."

"No amnesia?" she asked, almost crossing her fingers that there was, that Michael wouldn't remember her little flight from reality. It had only been a simple kiss after all. People did it all the time. Meant nothing. Wouldn't happen again. Except it shouldn't have happened in the first place, and it did mean something. That was the problem.

"Something you wish to forget?"

"More appropriately, someone."

"Ah, my Aleksandra is wrestling with affairs of

the heart at long last. I was about to give up hope, you know. But if that young man is anything like his mother, it's no wonder you're falling for him."

"I'm not."

"You don't lie very well. You never have, and I could always tell." He smiled. "You always had such a serious look on your face, and when you lied you were even more serious. And look at you now, twisting your hands the way you are."

Alek glanced down at her hands, and sure enough…

"And the frown on your face. If you keep it there too long, you know what will happen, don't you?"

Alek laughed. This was the same gentle scolding he'd always given her when she'd been a little girl. "A cold Alaskan wind will blow down from the Arctic and it will freeze the frown in place."

"And what would your young man think of that?"

"He's not my young man, Dimitri."

"But do you want him to be?"

"It's always easier staying blissfully uninvolved. No heartbreak, no worry, no distractions. And the truth is, I don't know if I want to stay uninvolved anymore. But as far as Michael's concerned, he's going to leave here soon, go back to his real life and a job that offers him so much more than we can here, so there's really no point in talking about him because he's just passing through. And he can't stay."

"Have you considered going with him when he leaves?"

She gave her head an adamant shake. "I'm not leaving here. Not unless you open the door and kick me out."

"Maybe I should, because sometimes I think you stay here for the wrong reasons. I think you find Alaska an easy place to hide."

"But I love this life. It's what I want to do, who I want to be, and that has nothing to do with Michael, and everything to do with me." And that much was true. But what Dimitri said was also true in part, as much as she hated to admit it. Living in an outlying area as she did made it easy to keep herself removed, and not only in the geographical sense. Uninvolved, but maybe not so contented with that anymore.

"But will you love this life as much when Michael leaves?"

Alek tucked her feet up under her and looked

out the window at the falling snow. "I do thrive here, you know." She laughed. "Of course, I suppose the definition of thriving is open to interpretation, isn't it?"

"So why do you stay, Alek? I know you love the work but you could do the work almost anywhere. Is it because of me? You don't want to leave me? If I were to go to Florida to retire to someplace warm, would you follow me there?"

"But you wouldn't," she argued.

"Probably not, but I could. And my life is changing now. Maggie might decide she prefers warm weather."

Alek didn't respond for a moment. Instead, she thought about her life without Dimitri. It would happen someday. She knew that. In one way or another they would be parted and she was prepared for that as much as anyone could be. "I'd stay here," she said, not at all as tentatively as she thought she would be about it. "I'd miss you terribly, and I'd have someplace nice and warm to visit, but I belong here, Dimitri, and it's not merely because of you."

"Well, I'd hate spending half my life sticky and sweaty," he muttered, pushing himself to the edge of the sofa. "But changes are inevitable, Aleksandra. Mine, yours… It was easier protecting you from them when you were a little girl, and maybe I protected you too much. But I can't protect you from them anymore."

"You and Maggie?"

He nodded. "At my age, I don't have time to sit about and ponder the changes. I have to act on them before it's too late."

"What about the money, Dimitri?" she asked. "That's why Michael is here, you know. He thinks you're being some kind of a cad about Maggie's resources, robbing her of her savings."

"What good son wouldn't?"

"Meaning you're not going to tell me?"

"Meaning Maggie asked me to keep a confidence, and I'll honor that. So don't put me in a position to choose, because I've already given my word, and I don't wish to hurt any feelings over this."

"My feelings?"

He nodded. "I love you with all my heart, but you're not the only one in it now. And it's nice after such a long time, making room for more. You ought to try it."

"I'm sure I'll love her after I know her better."

"Not for Maggie. I expect she'll find her place there in time, but I'm wondering if Michael shouldn't be finding a much larger place in your heart right now. After all, he does know that you talk in your sleep. And you do."

Dimitri disappeared out the door, leaving Alek alone on the sofa wondering about what he'd said. So maybe it was love. It could be, but she didn't know since she'd pretty much escaped it all these years. There'd been a few casual relationships—a date here and there, and then…

"He wants to see you," Mariska said, poking her head in the door. "The good-looking doctor…he said he wants to see you right away. Sure wish I had a good-looker like that wanting to see me right away, but all I have is Ivan, and good-looking…" She smiled fondly. "In his own way, I suppose. But nothing like yours."

"Tell him I'll stop in when I can." She wasn't anxious to see Michael, because the truth was, she didn't know what to expect, what to say, what to do. The easiest thing was simply to stay away until she did.

"Trying to play hard to get?"

"Trying *not* to be got," she replied with a disheartened sigh.

"Doesn't sound like much fun."

That much was true. It didn't. "Thanks for coming to find me," she said, trying not to sound too hard in her dismissal. Right now, though, she wanted to be alone. That was all.

Mariska took the hint and retreated into the hall, pulling the door shut behind her and leaving Alek by herself in the near-darkness. This was the better way. Not the easiest, but easy wasn't always the best option.

"The money?" Michael snapped. "You don't think it's any of my business?"

"You mind your money and I'll mind mine. That keeps it relatively simple, I think." Maggie pulled up a chair next to Michael's hospital bed and sat. "And my mental faculties are perfectly fine, thank you very much, so don't go getting any ideas to have me declared incompetent because I might turn the tables on you and have you declared incompetent."

"But it's not normal," he said, sitting up so he could get a better view of the door in case Alek decided to stop by. It had been hours since he'd asked for her, and so far, besides his mother and the nurse, the only other person he'd seen had been an old-timer who padded up and down the hall in his mukluks and a hospital gown, dragging his walker more than using it. "This isn't exactly a retirement destination, you know."

"And I'm not exactly retiring. Dimitri and I work well together, and I expect that I'll work as well with Alek, too."

"But you're—"

"Old," she interrupted. "Do you really think I'm too old to be useful?"

"Hell, no, I don't think you're too old. But I do think you're still rebounding from Dad's death. And I'm entitled to worry that you might be getting yourself into something you shouldn't."

"Practicing medicine in a small hospital where I'm truly needed is what you consider getting myself into something I shouldn't?" She shook her head impatiently. "I know you mean well for me, but this is my life and I'm not making any rash decisions. I want to be here. I want to be with Dimitri." A soft mellowness filled her voice. "And Dimitri wants to be with me."

"And your money," Michael snapped.

"You know what, Michael? Go home! Go back to your own life and quit interfering in mine, because I'm not changing the way things are here. I appreciate your concern, but I don't appreciate you butting in." Standing, Maggie leaned over the bed and gave him a motherly kiss on the forehead. "You're a skilled physician, but you really need to get a life of your own and let go of mine," she said, then left the room.

"She's a feisty one," Dimitri commented, stepping in seconds after Maggie had exited. "A lot like Alek, I think. Headstrong, full of ideas, passionate."

"I was beginning to wonder if we were going to talk," Michael replied stiffly.

"If your mother had her way, we wouldn't. That would be Alek's way, too. The women are conspiring to keep us apart. But it was inevitable since, in one way or another, I'm going to be part of Maggie's life now, which makes me part of your life, too."

"As in the one she's writing out all those checks to."

"That would be me, but I can assure you that it's not what you think."

"You sound like Alek. She assures me that it can't be what I think, yet no one will tell me otherwise so I'm left to think that you are taking advantage of my mother."

"And you are a good son for thinking so, and trying to protect her."

"Not good enough, since she's asked me to leave."

"And I'm asking you to stay a while longer."

Michael blinked back his surprise. "Why?" he asked, narrowing his eyes in suspicion as he looked up at Dimitri. "Why would you want me to stay?"

"Because I don't want to come between you and your mother, and I think you need time to work out your problems."

"My only problem with her is you."

Dimitri chuckled. "Your only problem with her is that she has moved on in her life. When my wife died, I didn't budge for a long time. It was easier to stay where I'd always been, but I had a force in my life that pushed me back into the world and made me stay there when I wanted to retreat. And I did. It's not easy, loving someone for as long as I did—as long as Maggie did—then losing them. But I was lucky because Alek was devoted. Probably too much. Maggie was lucky, too, because you were devoted. But devoted and possessive are two different things, Michael. I know you want to protect her, and I'm sure that if you keep pressuring her, in the end she'll give in and go back with you. That may be the best thing for you, but is it really the best thing for your mother?"

In spite of wanting to hate Dimitri, Michael found himself actually liking the man. He could see why his mother did, too. He had a forthright honesty about him. He was pithy and insightful, and if not for the fact that he was in possession of so much of his mother's money, Michael might have extended his hand to Dimitri in friendship. But there was still the issue of his mother's vulnerability and the possibility that Dimitri was exploiting it.

Of course, the two women he cared for most were absolutely devoted to Dimitri, which did tip the scales slightly. "I suppose we'll have to see how it works out, won't we?" Michael declared, his voice not quite so stiff as earlier.

"For Maggie's sake, as well as Alek's, I suppose we will."

"What's Alek got to do with this?"

"You love her, don't you?"

"What makes you think that?" Michael asked, not sure how to take this. Not even sure how to answer.

"You've been with her these past days. She's beautiful, intelligent, gifted." He chuckled. "You look at her like a man possessed. So how could that not be love?"

"Three days. That's how it could not be love. But even if I were developing some feelings, which I'm not admitting, it wouldn't matter because Alek would never love me back. She doesn't want to be involved and I think that prevails over anything else in her life."

"You could be right about that. But sometimes the best rewards are the hardest earned." He smiled tenderly as he talked about Alek. "You see her affection for me now, but it took me years to earn it. And it came little by little, sometimes in such small degrees I wondered if it would ever happen. But when it did, on that first time she crawled up in my lap and tugged on my beard, it was worth the wait. She's not easy, Michael. I know that better than anybody. But Aleksandra is well worth the wait, and something tells me you're not going to be standing in that line for very long."

Dimitri headed for the door. Once there, he turned back to Michael. "If you were to leave here a.m.a. tonight—" meaning against medical advice "—I would suggest that you go straight to a little cabin down the main road and find yourself a warm place with a hot-blooded Russian doctor and start fighting for that reward."

"I'm afraid that warm place might turn out to be chilly one," he replied.

"But chilly usually warms if you have the patience."

Michael listened to Dimitri's footsteps fade down the hall, then jumped out of bed, traded the hospital garb for his own, and ran to the closest exit. So far tonight Alek had ignored him, his mother had rebuked him and Dimitri had warned him. If he were smart, he'd run for the Jeep and get the hell out of Elkhorn, and leave the lot of them to their own little follies.

But for one brief moment in the airplane he'd

allowed himself to envision more with Alek than she wanted to give him. And he wanted that. For the first time in his life, he truly knew what he wanted.

"Don't get used to this," Alek warned her team as she hefted several tin plates outside with leftover scraps from her freezer. She'd cooked her dogs a hodgepodge of those unlabeled, unrecognizable frozen things—the dribs and drabs she'd frozen over the months with the full intention of pulling them out and eating them someday. All had been buried in a thick frost when she'd retrieved them, and she'd simply dumped them into a large pot to defrost them. "You know most dogs don't have it this good," she said, bending down to receive her fair share of licks and nuzzles from them.

"Most people don't, either," Michael commented from the back doorway.

"I thought you were to stay in the hospital tonight."

"And I thought you were coming to see me." He stepped back to let Alek pass by, then followed her through the kitchen. "I waited."

"I was busy."

"Which is just as well, because I finally had a talk with Dimitri. Nice man, as it turns out."

She shot him a surprised look. "And you two didn't beat each other up? Actually, I don't think you could take another good beating, and I think Dimitri would get the best of you. Good thing he took pity." The look in his eyes was so serious it scared her. She was so close to wanting him, but what she and Michael had would never go beyond that last kiss. "So, have you changed your mind about him?"

"Maybe, but I talked with my mother, too. I tried to, anyway, but she wouldn't say anything about it other than it's none of my business."

"Which is what Dimitri told me. As far as I'm concerned, that's the last of it."

"Which means I can leave here right now. Go back to Seattle and my job there. Forget all of this ever happened."

"If that's what you want." She straightened up, then wandered into the living room, thought about laying a fire for the night, then decided to turn up the propane heater. It was easier, and the fire would have been too cozy. Tonight, she didn't want cozy.

"*You* kissed *me*, Alek. What was that about? Because from where I was, it didn't seem like it was about you wanting me to leave here."

She shrugged, trying to put on an air of indifference. "One of those spur-of-the-moment things that happen, I suppose. Giving in to the moment. Overcome with relief." An impulse borne of something she would not allow to invade her thoughts.

"And that's all it was to you?"

"That's all," she lied, then turned away from him before he read that lie on her face. "No big deal."

"You know Dimitri doesn't want me to leave."

"That's what he told you?" she asked, staring out the front window to the desolate street. The snow wasn't particularly deep for October, but it got dark earlier now and people didn't wander out much. Michael shouldn't have come out because there was nothing here for him—not what he wanted.

"That, among other things."

She finally turned around to face him. "Well, the one thing you can always count on from Dimitri is that he's always going to tell you something. He's been telling me since I was seven, and it's never slowed down." She smiled fondly. "Sometimes he even tells you what you want to hear, but most of the time it's what you need to hear."

"You've lived with him that long? I guess I didn't realize that."

"Actually, he delivered me. He was the first person to ever lay eyes on me, and he never hesitates to remind me of that, especially when he wants something." Maybe a fire would be good after all. It was something to do, something to keep her busy. Grabbing a handful of tinder she kept in a basket on the opposite side of the room from the fireplace, Alek carried it over to the hearth and arranged it on the bottom of what would soon be her wood stack. Something else Dimitri had taught her. Start with the little things first then let them burn their way up to the big things. In a fire, as in life.

"So are you going to tell me?" Michael persisted. "I've been pretty open with you, and you haven't told me anything more than the fact that you're a..." He cut off his words.

"A what? A virgin? I was hoping you'd forgotten that, along with the kiss." She hadn't meant to say it, but she had. It didn't matter, though, because that much was true.

"Is that why you're so afraid of getting involved, Alek? Because you've never…?"

She shook her head. "Trust me, Michael. There are a lot of reasons to fear an involvement, but never having gone to bed with a man's not one of them."

"Then what it is, Alek? What keeps you so aloof? You act like you want to come near then when you get close you turn and skitter away like a frightened deer."

She grabbed up a few small logs then piled them in the fireplace, rearranged the kindling and struck a match. Just as she'd expected, the sparks caught and soon the fire was sufficient to burn on its own. When she was confident it would burn well, she walked over to the thermostat, switched down the heat and finally turned back to face Michael. "My mother was a mail-order bride. Someone my father sent off for. A prostitute, actually. She wanted America, but not Alaska, so she left before I was out of diapers, then my father, who didn't want a family—only a wife in his bed when he was home—fell off an ice cutter one night on a drunken binge and left me an orphan. Or abandoned by a mother who never came back for me, or however you want to look at it. The Romonovs took me in, but Olga wouldn't adopt me because of my dubious heritage. She was a proper lady and my mother was the prostitute wife of a drunken sailor. So you can't blame Olga for not wanting me."

She paused for a moment, trying to find the next words. Then she continued, "Dimitri doesn't know that I know about Olga, and I'd thank you not to tell him because it would break his heart."

"Of course I wouldn't," he said softly.

"He's always been so good to me, even when I pushed him away. And he never cared about my background the way Olga did. So that's my story. Alek Sokolov comes with rejection issues, and I reject before I can be rejected. It's not always the most pleasant way to live my life, but it works." The words came out so stiffly they didn't even sound like her, but once they were out she was totally drained, emotionally and physically, and all she wanted to do was go to bed, pull up the covers and wait for Michael to go away forever. Which he would now that he knew the worst of it. "Now that you know my deep, dark secrets, you can leave. Unless you still intend on going after Dimitri, in which case you can do it from somewhere other than my house." She pointed to the door. "Either way, get out!"

It had been an hour and she still hadn't heard him leave. Twice she'd dragged herself from bed to take a look out the window, but both times his Jeep was still there parked next to hers. What was he waiting for? For her to drop another ugly secret on him? Because there were no more. That was it. Everything she had in her little store.

Maybe she hadn't told him in the best way. Something other than a fit of temper would have been more proper. Have a nice civil chat over tea. *And, oh, Michael, by the way, let me tell you about my parentage.*

There really was no good way to put it. She'd overcome her lot in life thanks to Dimitri, but not her heritage. And she'd heard the snickers from the schoolchildren that she would turn out to be like her mother. That had been Olga's fear, too— the thing that had stopped her from having parents again. She'd overheard the discussions so many times, when Dimitri had wanted to adopt her and Olga had refused.

But to bring Michael into it? She shouldn't have, but for once in her life the need to be honest had far overcome the need to hide. And he deserved her honesty. Even if it didn't make any difference, anyway.

Alek shut her eyes for the twentieth time, hoping that sleep would come, but when it didn't she finally sat up, dropped her feet to the floor, and stood up—to pace.

"Walking in circles isn't going to make me go away," Michael called.

She didn't answer.

"You can walk all night, and unless you crawl out the window, you're going to have to come by me sometime."

Again, she didn't answer.

"And if you think you're the only one with parent problems…"

Alek threw open the door to the living room and glared at him. "What I told you isn't exactly a parent problem," she said tersely.

"But the fact that you think your parents make

you less worthy is a problem, Alek. You inherited their DNA but that doesn't have to control your life and, if anything, the way you've lived your life should show you that you're anything but less worthy. You are a strong woman, even though I'm not sure you know how much. And once you do know—know it deep down in your heart—you'll stop pushing people away because you're afraid you're not worthy of their love."

"And you're a psychiatrist now? You're going to put me down on the couch and analyze me? Well, you're wasting your time, Michael. I've been through analysis. I know what I'm about, and I'm able to be pragmatic about it. I am what I am. So are you happy? Not only do I bring a rich history of inherited family debauchery to the table, I have a psychiatric history as well. Which makes me a jolly ball of fun, don't you think?"

"It was Olga's loss that she never wanted you for a daughter. And you are Dimitri's daughter, in spite of it. So why are you so hard on yourself?" he asked. "You're intelligent, beautiful, successful…you have a man who adores you."

Her eyes softened. "He always has, even when I fought him. But me being here made his life hell when Olga was alive because they were always at odds because of me."

"I wasn't talking about Dimitri," he said gently.

"Don't!" she cried. "We can't."

"Can't what?"

"Can't anything, Michael. I mean, yes, I'm attracted to you. I might even have some feelings…"

"Might?"

"Okay, so I do have some feelings. But I don't want an involvement. Not now. Maybe not ever. It's too difficult."

"That's what you say, but I was kissed by someone who did want an involvement, Alek. I was there. Remember? Half that kiss was mine."

"You base so much on a kiss?"

"Because that's all I've had from you."

"I'm a virgin, remember?" she snapped. "I've given nothing to anyone, so don't think yourself special, because it was only a kiss."

"Only a kiss, *and* the truth. Which was so much more than a kiss. You know that, don't you, Alek? What you told me—"

"What I told you was the reason I don't get involved."

"That you're not worthy of being loved? That

you're afraid no one will? It's difficult when you won't allow them to, Alek. You do push people away…everyone but Dimitri. You keep your distance from your patients, keep your friends at an arm's length, like I saw you do that night in Beaver Dam, and never let anyone get too close."

Michael finally got up and crossed the room, then pulled her into his arms. She didn't go willingly, and she couldn't find it in her to relax into his arms, but the illusion of what this could be about felt so good. Before she even realized what she was doing, her arms were around him and her face was pressed to his chest. "My father told me my mother didn't want to be a mother and that's why she went away. I ruined that marriage, which started my father drinking and got him killed, and I came close to ruining Dimitri's marriage."

"You were a little girl, Alek. Everybody else involved in that situation was an adult and their decisions, however flawed, had nothing to do with the little girl and everything to do with their own personal needs. It wasn't you! It was never you!" He wrapped his arms even tighter. "You do want love, sweetheart, which is why you fight so hard against it. You want it but when it gets close you don't think you deserve it. And it's close, Alek. As close as you'll let it be. One day at a time, if that's what it takes."

She stiffened a bit, but didn't pull away. "I wanted to belong somewhere," she whispered. "That's all I ever wanted."

"And I wanted to be a better son to my father, but I couldn't because he sent me away from his deathbed when I was wiped out on amphetamines, and he told me not to come back until I was clean. He said that my mother deserved better than me for a son, and forbade me going near her until my filthy habit was cured."

"I'm so sorry," she whispered.

"So was I. I made bad choices, and my father made the only choice he thought he had. Neither of us got what we wanted and that's something that can't be changed."

"He died before you could make amends?"

Michael nodded. "When my mother—and my father—needed me most, I was off in drug rehab, dealing with the dependency and avoiding the issues. And I failed once, Alek. I went back to work, tried to pretend everything was normal, but then one little pill got in my way. Just for some sleep was what I told myself. But that night I couldn't sleep because my father was telling me to stay away from my mother until my filthy habit was cured. He'd been dead for six weeks, but he was still telling me, so the next morning I went back into rehab and finally confronted the whole ugly mess. I think that was when I really knew that some things cannot be changed, that we have to go on and make the best of what we have in spite of the mistakes and choices."

"For one pill? You went back for one pill?"

"One leads to two, and I didn't want to get to two."

She smiled weakly. "And now you're hell-bent on being the dutiful son?"

He chuckled. "Even when my mother doesn't want dutiful."

Alek took in a deep breath, and stepped away from him. "So what about us, Michael? The secrets are out but it doesn't really solve anything between us, does it? You have your problems and I have mine. How can all that ever be anything more than grueling for either of us?"

"Grueling? You really know how to cut to the

bottom line, don't you, Alek?" he said. "For God's sake, I'm trying to work it out with you, and all you do is tell me why we can't."

Earlier, Dimitri had said that sometimes the best rewards were the hardest earned. Problem was, he wasn't sure he was going to earn the reward no matter how hard he fought for it, because Alek had to fight for it, too. And he wasn't sure that she would.

"So tell me why we can, Michael," she whispered. "Tell me why, and how."

"I love you, Alek. That's all I can tell you. I do love you." He waited for her response, waited to hear her say that she loved him, too, because this was also her hard-earned reward, every bit as much as it was his. But she didn't, so he stepped away from her. "That's all I can say."

"And your holiday is over, isn't it?"

Instead of waiting for an answer, Alek returned to her room, locked her door, slid to the floor and wept for the first time since the day her father had died.

CHAPTER ELEVEN

IT WAS easier this way, Michael decided. He'd drive back to Nome, catch a commuter to Anchorage and be back in Seattle by that night, if all went well. Then tomorrow morning…well, he wasn't sure of it yet, but he'd already called his lawyer, so at least the gears were set in motion to release him from his contracts. That was the first step. The second was returning and fighting for Alek. He chuckled. Fighting Alek Sokolov to win Alek Sokolov. He was excited about that—a new life to live, new medicine to practice, and a love that would be well worth the effort. Although he wasn't kidding himself. She was going to take effort. "One day at a time, Alek. That's all I'm asking for. One day, with an option to negotiate the next."

If he'd said anything to her beforehand, she would have argued, run away, fought him off, or all three. So he hadn't. But soon he would, and he smiled, thinking over his return. Next time he came to Elkhorn he would stay, and put everything he had into the relationship—his heart, his soul, and the right amount of stubbornness—because that was what it was going to take to convince Alek that their life was meant to be together. And she did love him. He knew that, even though she was reluctant to see it or admit her own feelings. "And I've got all time in the world, Aleksandra Sokolov," he said as he sped down the icy roadway. "All the time and no place to go but back to you." And the medical practice he should have always been in. With Dimitri's blessing, of course, fighting for Alek and becoming part of the medical team at the Romonov clinic…even if he still wasn't clear about the situation between his mother and Dimitri. That, like his relationship with Alek, would have to be taken on faith. And today he had all the faith in the world that this new life was where he belonged, even if it was in Alaska.

Alaska… Well, that was another gamble, wasn't it? One thing was for sure—he was going to tackle it with better maps than he had. Of course, with a good map in hand he wouldn't have met Alek, or at least met her in the way he had. "Maybe I'll skip the map and let the pretty lady come to my rescue more often," he said, glancing up at Baranoff Pass looming ahead of him. Because, map or not, he was going to marry Alek. She didn't know it, and it was going to take some work to convince her she was worth it. But he would do it. How wasn't a given yet, but...

Up ahead. A movement. He squinted his eyes against the glare of the sun reflected off the west side of the massive Baranoff, and what he saw took almost a full second to register. Avalanche! It was a gentle slide, not at all what he would have expected. Almost like a wave...a great, white sweep of the slope sliding its way off the face and down over the pass.

Michael stared transfixed for another second as the snow continued its slide, then put the Jeep in gear, made a wide circle on the road, and raced back to Elkhorn, alternately trying his cell phone, which didn't transmit, and looking around him for any signs of another traveler.

But he was alone. And the slide was gaining momentum by the second.

"She'll need an X-ray," Alek told Eyanna, one of the nurses. "Just the elbow, although I don't think it's broken."

Ludmilla Popovich gave Alek an angry frown. "It's broken, young lady. I know a broken bone when I feel one." Ludmilla was nearly ninety now, and heartier than most people half her age. But she'd taken a tumble on the ice that morning. Of course, she'd gone to the mercantile afterward, darned a pair of woolen mukluks and baked a cake before she'd come to the clinic for a check. Priorities. And a sore elbow wasn't a priority in the life of Ludmilla. "And I want a sling. Can't be bothered with anything else."

Alek nodded, smiling. Life was normal again. That was probably a good thing, but she missed Michael already. That would pass, though. In time, it would pass, or at least dull. "And a sling you'll have," she told the old woman.

As Eyanna rolled Ludmilla down the hall in an olden wooden wheelchair, Alek looked out the front window in time to see Michael speed up to the front of the hospital and not come to a stop until he was well into the yard area. It was the outside pole light that stopped him, when he ran right over it. "What the…?"

Dropping her chart onto the table under the window, she ran to the clinic's front door, only to find Michael already inside and running down the hall. "What are you doing?" she shouted at him.

"Avalanche!" he gasped.

Not uncommon. Especially in the mountains…or the foothills. "Where?" she asked, not overly concerned since no one around here lived in an area where an avalanche would be expected.

"Baranoff Pass," he choked out. "Headed for the road over the pass, I think."

"Are you sure?" she gasped. "I've just had a snowboarding casualty in from up there." Her head immediately started swimming with the possibilities…more snowboarders, for starters. And where there were snowboarders there were snowmobilers.

He nodded. "It's what I saw, but I've never been up there…."

Without another word Alek broke into a run and didn't stop until she was standing on the front porch of Dimitri's cabin, with Michael standing behind her. "I'm going to have him start the alert," she called to Michael. "You go on back to my cabin and start getting my emergency packs from the shed out back." She took a deep breath. "How long?"

He glanced at his watch. "Less than five minutes."

She nodded. They were still on the good side of the time clock. At fifteen minutes things would start to shift, however. "Everything's marked and ready, so just get it out."

Michael nodded, then ran across the street as Alek pounded on Dimitri's door. Her first knocks brought no response so she opened the door. "Dimitri, Maggie!"

No response again, so she stepped inside, took a look around, then exited, perplexed. Maggie had a surgery in two hours so they couldn't have gone far. She looked up and down the street as she ran toward her cabin, and people who'd heard about the avalanche were beginning to wander out of their houses to get organized. They knew the timeline, too, and it didn't take long to get a rescue response under way. "I'm going up on first response," she shouted at Mariska, who was running up the street after her. "Call Walter, and see if he can find someone to get up in the air." Normally, that's what she did while Dimitri went out, but Dimitri wasn't here and she didn't have time to hunt him down.

"I've already made the calls," Mariska yelled breathlessly, as she followed Alek around the cabin. "Eyanna's on the shortwave right now, trying to find out if we have casualties up there."

"When Dimitri comes back, which he should as soon as he hears about it, tell him I'm going in with my team, and Michael's going in with me. Dimitri should be on radio, so let him know, unless he hears from me, not to come up but to stay put and handle the casualties we send down." She glanced at her watch. According to Michael's timeline, they were at seven minutes.

"How are we getting there?" Michael asked, bringing the last of the emergency packs out of the shed. Before Alek could answer, Mariska pulled the tarpaulin off the dogsled next to the shed and started piling on the packs while Alek began to hitch up the team.

"Have you ever done an avalanche response?"

Alek asked him. "Outside of teaching it, I mean. Have you ever gone on a rescue?"

He nodded. "But not the first response."

"Well, I'm going in by sled, and you go by snow machine. Stay wide of me and let me lead since I know the way." She tilted back her Cossack cap and looked up at him, her eyes filled with worry. "Baranoff's not normally unstable, but we've had fluctuating weather so there's no telling what we're going to get into." She grabbed a pack from the pile and handed it to him, along with a collapsible probe pole. "That's your basic equipment—shovel, transmitter, AvaLung…" A vest device with an emergency breathing apparatus that would allow air to be extracted from the snow for up to an hour through a breathing tube, if all conditions were optimal.

He nodded without saying anything as he strapped on his pack and piled his equipment onto the snowmobile. Then, before he climbed on, he pulled Alek into his arms and held her for a instant. "See you up at the top," he said roughly.

"Up at the top," she replied. She hesitated, then pulled his face down for a brief kiss. "And down at the bottom afterward." Then she put on her goggles, tugged up a scarf to cover her mouth, hopped on her sled and was off. Her dogs were trained to short, verbal commands, and as she shouted "Forward!" she looked back over her shoulder at Michael. She did love him so much.

She'd done this before. Many, many times. Sometimes things turned out well, sometimes they didn't. Most often, though, the victims were novices in the snow, people who didn't recognize the warning signs…precipitation, wind, a weak snow layer, unstable settlement. Sometimes they were people who did know the snow but either got sloppy, too confident or simply played the odds. Baranoff wasn't as predictable as it once had been… Alaska was warming, great ice floes were breaking up, mountains of snow like Baranoff were giving way. "We've got time," she said as the dogs pulled her efficiently and quickly along the snow-packed trail to the north, barking their excitement at the expedition.

Alek glanced back to see Michael keeping up—he was driving in a wide sweep out to the side and slightly behind her, so as not to distract the dogs. And to stay far enough away that if the avalanche progressed, or a new one started, he would be out of the sweep that would catch her. He waved at her once, then surged behind a clump of pines, and she held her breath until she could see him again. More than she'd ever known could be possible, Michael was in her heart.

He was her heart, and later, when this was all over, she would tell him.

As her lead husky barked his warning of an upcoming tree, Alek shifted her focus abruptly to the rescue and gave the command for the team to turn. By the time they reached Baranoff, others would be mobilized, and an air team would have been deployed, probably from Nome. "Right," she shouted to her dogs, who made the next turn without a waver. Michael made the same turn a little way back, and as Baranoff loomed ahead of them, Alek went over the procedures in her mind—start with a beacon-guided search, then do a surface and scuff search, meaning look for signs of life or anything that would indicate someone has been through there recently. She and Michael would walk the area in a zigzag path until other help arrived, then they would do parallel sweeps, back and forth. "Other help," she choked. Dear God, she hoped that wouldn't be necessary.

Ahead, she could see the great Baranoff casting its shadow. It was the divide that separated the Arctic from the sub-Arctic, and she'd loved to come up here with Dimitri when she'd been a child. She'd loved it best when the sun dipped below the horizon and the glow of the evening shone like glitter scattered across all the snowy mountain peaks that could be seen only from the top of Baranoff. It was a golden world, filled with a child's amazement over how the white snow could take on such a new, vibrant life in blues and pinks and golds, and she'd always begged Dimitri to build her a house up here so she could always look out over this world she considered all her own, and never, ever have to come down.

Right now, though, Baranoff was ugly, and the closer she got the more her stomach lurched. Finally, when she'd reached the base and knew the rest of the way in was by foot, she climbed off the sled, ran to the bush line and immediately started a visual scan, along with homing in her transceiver, hoping that if anyone had been up here, they'd been smart enough to carry a transmitter.

"We're still on good time," Michael said, running up behind her. "Less than fifteen minutes since I saw it. So are you ready to go in?"

Alek gave him a grim nod, never once taking her eyes off the snow field ahead. She was already searching for any sign that someone needed to be rescued. "Over there," she said, pointing to an area that was parallel to the road running through the pass. "Something in the snow." As she said that, her stomach gave another lurch.

Michael pulled up his binoculars and took a look. "Can't tell for sure. It might be a ski pole, or maybe something shiny off a snowboard or snow-mobile. It's metallic, but there's not much…"

Before his words were out, Alek was making her way across by foot. Halfway to the object, she turned to find Michael coming up from another direction. They converged on the spot at the same time.

"Snowmobile," she said, looking down at the blade. It wasn't buried deeply, and she dropped to her knees to scoop away the snow. "Begin a pinpoint search, using the snowmobile as your start position." A pinpoint search involved sweeping the transceiver over the snow from side to side, back and forth. "And I'm going to do a spot probe." Probing areas where victims might have escaped to, such places as the base of a tree or nearby rock. In the distance, the sound of emerging rescue teams split the unnatural still-ness of the area, but Alek didn't take her focus off digging through the snow at the snowmobile in case someone was buried down there.

"I'm not going to lose you," Michael said quietly, as he set his transceiver to maximum volume. "I know this isn't the time, Alek, but I'm not going to lose you."

She looked up long enough to smile, then went back to her work. "You're not going to lose me, Michael," she said, scooping away the snow. "I promise, you're not…" What she saw on the side of the buried iron dog choked away the rest of her words. *Iron Doc*.

This was Dimitri's snowmobile.

"Are you getting a signal?" she choked, backing away and gentling her probe pole down into the snow.

"Nothing."

"How much time?"

"Just a little over fifteen. I think we're probably still okay, but..." He turned around and saw that Alek's face was as white as the snow. "What?" he asked.

She pointed to the snowmobile. "Dimitri's."

"Are you sure?"

She nodded, too numb to speak.

If Dimitri was out here, then his mother... Michael swallowed back a hard lump in his throat. "Listen, sweetheart. We're going to find them. Just expand your search." At a time when he needed to be closer to Alek, to pull her into his arms and hold her, he stepped even further away. This was no time to quit, no time to slow down. In another fifteen minutes the odds would be against a rescue and the rescue would, without a spoken order, turn to a body recovery. "Do what you do, Alek. Don't think about anything but the rescue. Do you understand?"

"Yes," she whispered, pulling out her probe then putting it back in another spot.

Two minutes later, after crisscrossing a wide span of the immediate search field without any luck, they moved their search north and did the same. By the time they'd moved on to the third, then fourth fields, other rescuers were already joining the search, stretching out in the areas he and Alek had not yet covered. Friends, strangers, old, young… When the word went out, nobody hung back. Those who couldn't search stayed on the ready with warm blankets and hot drinks that seemed to materialize from nowhere; those who could search simply did what they knew how to do without being told. Amazing teamwork— something he'd never taught in his classes, or experienced in person.

But it was that teamwork that would rescue his mother and Dimitri. He trusted that, and counted on it. Michael glanced at his watch. Time was critical now.

"The whole area of the slide is relatively small in circumference," Ivan Petrovich, Mariska's husband, shouted as he approached Michael. "I've heard from the pilot that there's no sign of life, at least not from the air."

Michael nodded as he looked back at the snowmobile. Alek was still searching, but she had circled out now, meaning she'd given up hope that Dimitri was near the snowmobile. "Come on, Maggie. Don't do this to me," he choked as he continued, one slow, cautious step at a time, listening, listening…

Alek stopped for a second to survey the area. Right now, at least fifty people were walking the same steps, doing the same probe, and word was out that Dimitri might be buried, which made the efforts even more frantic. And with Dimitri… Alek chanced a glance at Michael. He knew Maggie would be with Dimitri, but he hadn't said a word. Instead, he'd continued like everyone else, intent in what they were doing and determined to bring this to a good end. Except they were drastically out of time now.

"It's Dimitri," she told herself as she turned in a full circle. "Dimitri…" Raising her hand to visor her eyes, Alek looked at the little ledge where they'd picnicked at times. It was an easy climb, but to a young girl, it had seemed an awesome one because it had seemed so high. She'd towered over the world up there, and the two of them would spend the afternoon playing chess, of all things. They would eat sandwiches and play, sometimes well into the evening, and afterward she'd always…

Alek sucked in a sharp breath. She'd always climbed down the ledge into the tiny cave—one that fit her and barely fit Dimitri. "Michael!" she shouted. "Over there." She pointed to the area underneath the ledge as she started to trudge through the snow.

"What?" he shouted.

"The cave. I think they're in the cave." Packed in by the snow and possibly suffocating!

Michael reached the cave before she did, as did several of the men, and they were busy digging with their hands by the time she fell to her knees in the snow in the shadow of the ledge and shut her eyes to pray. If they weren't here… There was a shout and a renewed flurry of activity near the cave. Then more indistinct yelling.

"They've found him! He's in there with Maggie," Michael called. "He's shouting something awful," he said a few seconds later. "Something about not leaving here without his buzhenina."

"They've found him?" she whispered, her voice trembling.

"Almost. They're in there, and Dimitri is being rather vocal about directing his rescue. So, what is this buzhenina he refuses to leave?"

Alek took in a deep, ragged breath, pushed back her Cossack cap and fell into Michael's arms. "A ham," she said, as the tears started to flow. "He must have gone over the pass to Elim Ost's to get a ham."

"On a snowmobile with my mother?"

"That's the best way to get there." She swiped at her tears and laughed in relief. "A stupid ham."

Five minutes later she was still in Michael's arms as first Maggie and then Dimitri were carried from the cave. Michael ran to his mother as Alek ran to Dimitri, who was clutching his bu-zhenina with one hand and waving to his rescuers with the other, as if he was on parade. He was probably already telling the tales of his day in the avalanche. As a round of cheers went up, Alek gave Dimitri a kiss on the forehead, tugged on his beard affectionately, as she'd done when she'd been a child, then returned to the search field in case anyone else was buried. The hard tears she wanted to cry would come later, but right now there was work to be done. Halfway back to the area, Michael caught up to her, took her mittened hand in his, and they went on, together.

* * *

This was the fifth time she'd heard the story, but she wanted to hear it again and again. Sitting here next to the hearth wrapped in Michael's arms, listening to Dimitri tell the tale and watching him hold on to Maggie… Alek let out a contented sigh because she was contented. No one else had been involved. No injuries, no deaths. Everyone was safe and all was well.

"It was the crack," Dimitri boomed. "If you've lived your life here like I have, you know what it means." He chuckled. "It means run like hell. And that damn iron dog just wouldn't back down there fast enough. So we did what you're supposed to do. We got off, stayed on the high slope and ran across to the side. I always knew Alek's cave was good for something."

"More like a hole in the wall," Maggie commented as she sipped her hot tea. "Barely big enough for the two of us."

"But I kept telling her my Aleksandra would figure it out. She would remember the cave."

"And your Aleksandra has a good mind to throw that buzhenina away," Alek said, smiling.

"Then I'll have to go get another." Dimitri reached over and took Alek's hand and gave it a squeeze. "Or send you over by airplane since I don't think I'm going to wander away too far for a while." Letting go of her hand, he rubbed his broken arm, the only injury to either of them. It had happened when the snowmobile had tipped and the transmitter had broken. "And I don't mind telling you, I think I'm getting too old for this. Maybe it's time to settle down with a good woman and think about retiring in another ten or fifteen years."

"Well, I think it's time to go over and do rounds at the clinic," Alek said, pushing herself off the floor. "As much as I hate to leave good company…" She looked down at Michael, smiling. "Duty does call."

"Mind if I tag along?" he asked, following her out the door.

"Are you sure? I thought maybe you'd rather stay closer to your mother tonight."

"She's got Dimitri, and I'd rather stay close to you," he said, taking her hand. "Tonight, tomorrow night, and the night after that…"

Alek didn't say anything for another minute. Instead, she listened to the crunch of the snow underfoot, a sound she'd always loved, and loved even more now that her crunch was amplified by Michael's. "I was so scared," she said. "You always know it can happen, but I never…"

"One day at a time," he said, stopping next to his rental Jeep, which was still sitting in the front yard of the clinic, with the light pole still crushed underneath it. "That's the best any of us can do, Alek."

"And even then, it's not enough, is it?" She skimmed her hands along the side of his Jeep, and at the passenger's door she stopped and turned to face him. "Will you stay, Michael? I know I don't have the right to ask you, especially after the way I've been, but this is one day and I don't want to face the next one without you. And you know I come with a whole set of problems…"

"Not so many as you think," he said, cupping her face in his gloved hands. "Not so many that we can't work through them together."

"I'm always going to have a temper," she warned. "And be stubborn and opinionated."

"And I'm always going to be much better at charming people," he countered, smiling. "And an occasional moose when it's necessary," he said, then pointed to one that was standing in the middle of the road, simply staring at them.

"As long as she doesn't have love in her eyes, that's fine with me."

"But do you, Alek?' he asked seriously. "Do you have love in your eyes?"

"I did, the first day you walked across the lecture stage in Seattle. You just took my breath away, Michael. I mean, you had the same passion I did for wilderness medicine, and even from the back row I could hear it, see it. Everything I felt for you got tarnished a bit, but it never went away, because I think I probably loved you then, or at least had a crush big enough to turn into love, and I do love you now. I'm a little afraid of it, and I'm not very good at it, but, no matter what, I'll always love you." Saying the words wasn't so tough as she'd thought it might be. No fear of rejection, no fear of anything except spending a life without him.

He pulled her roughly into his arms. "And the past is the past, Alek? No going back there?"

"As far as I'm concerned, there's only future, which is going to start…" She wiggled out of his embrace, pulled up her coat sleeve and looked at her watch. "In about ten minutes."

"What happens in ten minutes?" he asked.

"It's going to take me ten minutes to do my rounds then after that, Doctor, I do have one issue left to resolve. It's a dreary little condition called…" She pulled him down to whisper in his ear. "Virginity. Is there something in your little bag of wilderness medicine that will cure it?"

Michael chuckled as he pulled her back into his arms. "Not in an igloo, I hope!"

Six months later

"I can't believe all the space!" Alek exclaimed, stepping into the brand-new surgery. "It's incredible. And the new patient wards… What you've done here, Maggie! It's amazing!"

"Four doctors practicing in one hospital needed more space," Maggie said. "I told Dimitri from the start that I was going to expand the place if he intended keeping me here, and that's when there were three of us. Of course, I hoped that once you and Michael met—"

"To which I told her *absolutely* no," Dimitri interrupted, then chuckled. "No to the extension, not to Michael and Alek. I thought *that* sounded like a pretty good idea. But when Maggie talked about all these additions and I refused, she sent me that damned check for the contractor anyway."

"And when he refused, I knew he meant business," Maggie supplied. "But I told him that was the only way he was going to get me to Alaska permanently. He had to take the offer. And I kept it a secret because I knew a certain very possessive member of my family would be totally opposed to having me start a new life and I really was trying to be quiet about working it out, which, apparently *didn't* work out. But that turned out to be a very good thing."

"She's a mean one when it comes to negotiations," Dimitri added, scowling. "Wants her own way, gets grumpy when she doesn't get it. And opinionated… Dear lord, the woman is full of opinions."

"And my opinion now is that we should get on with the party," Maggie said, blowing a kiss to Michael. "Now that we are officially four instead of three, and Michael is here for good, instead of flying up whenever he could get away, or Alek flying down whenever she could. So it's time to celebrate."

"Five," Alek said quietly.

"Five what?" Dimitri asked, arching his bushy eyebrows.

Michael leaned to give Alek a kiss, then straightened up and said, "My mother said now that we're officially four instead of three, but it's actually five instead of three."

"At last!" Dimitri boomed. "My daughter is giving me that grandchild at last." He chuckled. "Of course, I knew that. What good father doesn't know when his daughter is pregnant? She glows, like my Aleksandra has for the past weeks. Glows, looks happy, smiles." He pulled a piece of paper from his pocket and handed it to Alek. "A little gift for the celebration," he said.

Alek opened the paper and read the words. At first they didn't sink in, but then… "You've adopted me?"

"Much too late," he said seriously. "I should have done it when you first came to live with us, but I…I never got around to it." He would never speak a word against his wife, which was the way it should have been. "It would have made your life better, I think. And after Olga was gone, I thought you were too old for such a thing. Then

Michael and I had a little father to future son-in-law talk the day you were married and, well, it's only a token, but you are my daughter, Aleksandra, in every way that a man could have a daughter. And I hope this doesn't seem like a silly gesture from a foolish old man to finally make it official."

"Not silly." Alek sniffled back a tear, and smiled first at Michael, then Dimitri. "And if I have a son, I suppose you want me to name him Dimitri?"

"Dimitri Michael, Michael Dimitri. Either way is good."

Maggie gave Dimitri's arm a meaningful shove. "We've got people waiting for gouryevskaya kasha," she said, heading toward the door. "And buzhenina."

Dimitri turned to Alek. "You fixed buzhenina?"

She shook her head and pointed to Michael.

"You fixed buzhenina?" he asked Michael.

"And pelmeni with draniki," Michael said, giving his wife a wink.

Dimitri opened wide his arms. "Son!" he boomed. "It's good to have you home."

Michael wrapped his arm around Alek's

waist and pulled her close to him. "And it's good to be home."

"It's good to be home," Alek whispered, placing her hand over Michael's as he laid it on her belly. "So very good."

MEDICAL ROMANCE™

 **Large Print**

Titles for the next six months…

February

THE SICILIAN DOCTOR'S PROPOSAL	Sarah Morgan
THE FIREFIGHTER'S FIANCÉ	Kate Hardy
EMERGENCY BABY	Alison Roberts
IN HIS SPECIAL CARE	Lucy Clark
BRIDE AT BAY HOSPITAL	Meredith Webber
THE FLIGHT DOCTOR'S ENGAGEMENT	Laura Iding

March

CARING FOR HIS CHILD	Amy Andrews
THE SURGEON'S SPECIAL GIFT	Fiona McArthur
A DOCTOR BEYOND COMPARE	Melanie Milburne
RESCUED BY MARRIAGE	Dianne Drake
THE NURSE'S LONGED-FOR FAMILY	Fiona Lowe
HER BABY'S SECRET FATHER	Lynne Marshall

April

RESCUE AT CRADLE LAKE	Marion Lennox
A NIGHT TO REMEMBER	Jennifer Taylor
THE DOCTORS' NEW-FOUND FAMILY	Laura MacDonald
HER VERY SPECIAL CONSULTANT	Joanna Neil
A SURGEON, A MIDWIFE: A FAMILY	Gill Sanderson
THE ITALIAN DOCTOR'S BRIDE	Margaret McDonagh

MILLS & BOON®

Live the emotion

0107 LP 2P P1 Medical

MEDICAL ROMANCE™

Large Print

May

THE CHRISTMAS MARRIAGE RESCUE Sarah Morgan
THEIR CHRISTMAS DREAM COME TRUE   Kate Hardy
A MOTHER IN THE MAKING   Emily Forbes
THE DOCTOR'S CHRISTMAS PROPOSAL   Laura Iding
HER MIRACLE BABY   Fiona Lowe
THE DOCTOR'S LONGED-FOR BRIDE Judy Campbell

June

THE MIDWIFE'S CHRISTMAS MIRACLE Sarah Morgan
ONE NIGHT TO WED   Alison Roberts
A VERY SPECIAL PROPOSAL   Josie Metcalfe
THE SURGEON'S MEANT-TO-BE BRIDE Amy Andrews
A FATHER BY CHRISTMAS   Meredith Webber
A MOTHER FOR HIS BABY   Leah Martyn

July

THE SURGEON'S MIRACLE BABY   Carol Marinelli
A CONSULTANT CLAIMS HIS BRIDE   Maggie Kingsley
THE WOMAN HE'S BEEN WAITING FOR
                                        Jennifer Taylor
THE VILLAGE DOCTOR'S MARRIAGE Abigail Gordon
IN HER BOSS'S SPECIAL CARE   Melanie Milburne
THE SURGEON'S COURAGEOUS BRIDE   Lucy Clark

MILLS & BOON®
Live the emotion

0107 LP 2P P2 Medical